Shane

Dragon
Savior
Book 4

KATHI S. BARTON

This is a work of fiction. Names, characters, places, and incidents are products of the author's imagination or are used fictitiously and are not to be construed as real. Any resemblance to actual events, locations, organizations, or persons, living or dead, is entirely coincidental.

World Castle Publishing, LLC
Pensacola, Florida
Copyright © Kathi S. Barton 2016
Paperback ISBN: 9781629895260
eBook ISBN: 9781629895277
First Edition World Castle Publishing, LLC, August 22, 2016
http://www.worldcastlepublishing.com

Licensing Notes
Cover: Karen Fuller
Editor: Maxine Bringenberg

Prologue

"Tonight, we will rid the world of another witch. Their magic, their unholy ways of making others do what they wish, their worshipping of Satan, will be abolished with them one at a time, so long as we have breath in our bodies to do so." Rohm Herald looked out over his followers, men who believed as he did, that witches and their kind should not be allowed to be a part of this world. He turned to look at the witch on the stake behind him, at her face and then her belly, fat, no doubt, with Satan's bastard no matter what she said to the contrary. Her lies had brought her here, and she would die knowing that he'd done all he could to bring her from the darkness this night. "Do you give yourself over to His word? Do you now forsake the lifestyle that you have lived, following the man with a forked tongue and black magic?"

For an answer, she spit in his face. He wished they were

alone even now. He would wipe that smile from her face even as he cut her heart out. Rohm drew back his hand to slap her, to bloody her blasphemous lips once again.

"You do and you will never see your next child take its first breath. Mayhap you won't anyway, if I can help it." The words, spoken softly, felt as if she'd burned them into his head. "You will stop this foolishness, Rohm Michael Herald, or I will bring a curse down on you that will be felt generations down your line. So far removed from you that you will think I lie, that my magic has no meaning to you."

"Are you saying that you be a witch?" She laughed then, her head thrown back in a mirth that made his body tighten in fear and anger. "You will die this day, by fire, should you not tell me that you have no magic in you, that you do not practice the arts of witchcraft if you be one. Renounce now and I will spare you the death of fire."

"I will die anyway, and you know that. You have it in your head that I will, and that will come to pass. Even my babe, your grandchild, is going to die with me because you care not to hear the truth of my words." He did know that, but he would make her death quick, much quicker than that which was planned. "I am a witch."

His congregation gasped at her words. Then when she laughed, the sound of it echoing over the vast field that they had been using for a year now to rid the world of women such as her, once again Rohm felt the stirring of fear settle over him.

Rohm had no choice in this now. She had made her decision and now she must die by it. Lifting the flame that had been handed to him by his second, his own son, Michael, he turned to the men that had worked with him for so long. It was coming up on midnight, the bewitching hour, he'd been told; time to do his duty for the world.

"Tonight we bring to our fold Mary Wayne. She has been found guilty of being a witch; has admitted to us all here that she is what we feared, the child of Satan." Mary laughed behind him and began speaking, her voice too low for him to understand her words. Raising his own voice, Rohm continued. "We burn the devil from her and his child within her. Then when it is done, and all is balanced in this world, we will give her body a proper burial and bless her for her life. For being a mere woman, she knows not what she has done."

The sound of her words came to him then. She was cursing him, and those that were in the field beyond. When he turned to her again, the flame ready to set to the wood there, the moon was blotted out for a moment. He staggered back when two great beasts landed in the field with them. But as he made his way to them, thinking the beasts were there to eat them, a man appeared in the place of one of them, a woman by his side in place of the other. Rohm thought perhaps it was his mind playing tricks on him, or maybe the witch making him see things that were not there. The man and woman were close enough to make out now, and he nearly welcomed them.

As soon as the flame in his hand went out, the men that he could call upon fell to their knees, then to their backs as the man and woman walked by them. They had surely killed them, he thought. And would him as well. Soon it was just the four of them, Mary, the couple, and himself. Rohm felt his body tighten and his skin crawl when he dared to think what this might mean. They too were witches, powerful ones that had come to murder him.

"Mary, you've gotten yourself into trouble again, haven't you?" The witch called the man his lordship. "Rohm. I can see that you have not heeded the advice of others, and have perhaps bitten off a bit more than you can chew in this. You were told to stop killing the women that will not heel to your word. And that burning women at the stake isn't the way things are done. Were you not?"

"She has claimed boldly to be a witch. Has admitted before my men that she is indeed a practitioner of the dark arts. In this, she has left me no choice but to do as my fellow believers wish and burn the devilry out of her." Mary claimed that she had not. "I heard you. You said you were a witch."

"She is a witch, but does not wholly practice the dark side of it." Rohm backed up when the man, a great warrior, stepped up on the dais of stone set up for him to stand upon when Rohm himself was at his duties. He looked to be a man of great wealth and size. His body was lean, not an ounce of fat upon him, Rohm thought, not at all like he was. "But it's not the reason that you've brought her here, is it? You've got another agenda that has nothing to do with dark or white magic, but with her babe and your son. You should learn more about witchcraft and the people who use it if you plan to use it against them. Dark arts are—"

"Anthony, he cares not what they practice," the woman said with an air of authority. "Nor does he care if she is indeed a witch or not. Others have not done as he told them, and he's found reason, much like he has with Mary here, to have them killed. Mary has done nothing to him, save not telling him sooner that it is his own son who is the father of her unborn child. It is only happenstance that she is also a witch." Anthony turned to the woman at his side and smiled at her. Rohm could almost taste their love for each other, feel it as if it were a warmed blanket that had been dried on the line in the yard. And it pissed him off. Women were not to show such emotions to a man, especially not in public as this one was doing. He'd opened his mouth to call her a witch as well when she simply looked at him. His throat grew tight and he could not speak. But she could. "Come, the night grows cold and we have much to do this night."

"So we do." Anthony turned to the witch, and with a snap of his fingers she was down on her knees in front of the stranger. "Mary, I have a task for you should you like. If you've no wish, there will be no punishment and you will be well paid for your troubles this night."

"He meant to kill me, my lord. I feel it my duty to end his life where he stands. I am here only because his son, Michael, could not keep his pecker in his pants when he has a wife of his own." Anthony looked out over the field, and Rohm knew the exact moment that Anthony spied his son. "He will need to pay for what he has had done to me this night. I have no house, my books have been burned, and he has taken my coin as well."

"Do not think to harm my son, sir. I know not who you are, but should you harm him, I will find you and make you pay." Anthony looked at him then, and Rohm felt his body burn with the desire to run and never look back. "He is my only son. You will not harm him."

"Nay, I will not harm him." Rohm felt the air rush from his body then. But it was short lived as the man continued. "But he will not live to see his next child born, nor will you, I fear. You both have been found out, I think. His wife and your own lady wife know of the bastards that you have sired. There is a lot going on at your house this night."

Rohm looked at Mary and could see her head bent, her body shaking with laughter. When he reached for her, his knife in his hand before he could think how close the man was, Rohm decided that he would kill the witch himself. But his body grew hard till he could not even blink when the man told him to stop. The command in his voice, as hard as the stone he stood upon, held Rohm there. Then the man helped Mary up till the witch now stood near the woman and the man as he spoke.

"As I have mentioned, we've a task for you should you like to take it. It will be one of great importance to me and my family. It concerns the babe that you now carry." Rohm watched as the woman touched her hand to Mary's bastard child. Did they not know how unclean she was? Did she even care what she was doing? That inside of her grew a child that was made in sin? But he could no more speak to them than he could move. He could only watch in horror as they moved away and out of his reach.

This is not to be, he thought. He was in charge of clearing the world of such things as witches and other things that he did not understand. He cared not for what they had to say, but it was his duty, as a man of the cloth, to do this thing. For now, there was little to nothing he could do. But he would rise again, and soon. Rohm had lost this battle, but he would find her again.

As the midnight hour passed over, then the sun began to rise up and over the mountain, Rohm could finally begin to move. His body was sore, stiff from lack of movement. But his mind, his plans for the woman and man, and even Mary, had been plotted out. He would be ready for them; he would have his revenge in this.

He would find them. Even if he had to do so on his own, he would find them and kill them for what they'd done to him this night. When the men with him began to move, standing and looking bewildered, Rohm started barking out orders. He wanted this done, he wanted them dead. His next grandchild was due to be born in a matter of weeks.

"Find Mary, bring her back to me."

No one questioned what had happened to her, where she had gone if not up in flames, but moved as if they were in a trance, their bodies as stiff and sore as his. But when one of the men called to him, told him that something had gone wrong, he knew with each step he took that his son, Michael, had died this night, and by the hand of, if not the witch, then the man and woman with her.

His son, the only living legitimate son of his loins, lay where he had dropped, his body fat with laziness, his face relaxed in death. Leaning over his child, he touched his fingers to his face and found him to be cold, as cold as the ground that would soon welcome him.

Rohm thought that nothing could have prepared him for the pain of it. It rolled over him in waves of anger, sorrow, and hate. The feeling in his heart blackened, killing whatever peace and good will he'd had there.

Rohm's son had been born to him late in life, his wife having given him nine girls, all of them useless. She had gone to her own cold grave when she'd finally done her duty and given him a son. So happy he was with his namesake that Rohm never saw his wife die, leaving the room as soon as his child was given to him. Rohm couldn't even say if she had been dead long when he'd taken his child to the church to be baptized, having him blessed in the event that something befell him too. He had wanted to take no chances with this boy. He thought that blessing him so soon after his birth would prevent him from being sickly and dying.

"Lord Herald, what should we do now?" He looked over at the wood piled high yet unburned by flame. The stake that he himself had cut down and put in the ground stood in testimony to the fact that he had failed. "Shall we take young Michael to the undertaker now?"

"Yes. And tell my eldest daughter...." He couldn't remember her name, not that he would have tried had he even known it. "Tell her that I said to prepare a feast for his wake. When he is buried, it is then that we will find this woman and man and bring them here for their crimes against us. Mary will pay for my son and all the other sins that she has heaped upon my door."

"Man and woman, Lord Herald?" He had no idea how to describe them, so sending them on their way to take care of his child, he moved to his dais and sat upon it. The words of the man and of the witch came back to him. He would not see the birth of his next grandchild.

~~~

Anthony wasn't sure what to make of the woman that walked with them. She wasn't rude really, but she was too blunt for his taste, then she would act as if she were wounded and stupid if you called her out about it. It was difficult to keep up with her conversation as well, which was flying from one thing to the next like something bouncing in a room. And he knew from what they'd been able to see in the future that she wasn't to be trusted, not even with this task, but she would not have much say in what they needed of her. She need only to give birth, that was all. The rest would work itself out. When his own lady wife told him to stop his thoughts and behave, he thought that he'd been very good in not taking her backside with his hand and showing the witch how to behave.

Eve, the heart of his body, her own body heavy with their children, looked as beautiful to him as did the sun setting over his castle. But they had seen what their future would be and had decided to take care that things were prepared for their children, children that they'd never see or meet should things come to pass as they were shown to them. This woman, one of many, would help them in that. She wasn't as good as the others nor as magical, but needed all the same. Mary was the first of their tasks to set into motion, and Anthony was worried that they'd made a mistake in her.

You know as well as I that we have not. And it is not the woman that we're depending upon, but her child. He looked at Eve when she spoke to him through their link. *Mary's daughter, she will be the key to many doors that will open that will save our children.*

I know that, my love, but I do not have to like her much. She need only to understand what she is to do and when to do it. I fear, as I can feel that you do as well, that she is not up for the task. I worry for her part in this. If she does not heed our warnings and stay where we put her, then she will die, and her child as well. She assured him that Mary would do well. *I hope so. I should hate to think of her failing them in their hours of need.*

His wife told him that Mary would not fail. There was little doubt that she was to have a babe and that it would be a daughter. The rest had already been set in motion, and she need only to live long enough to bear the child. Eve patted his hand, then turned back to Mary to tell her of what they needed.

"Mary, we know that you have magic, but not a great deal of it. You can cast spells that come to pass, but other than that, you have nothing more." Mary opened her mouth, but his lovely mate only raised her hand to stay her words. "I will not listen to you puff yourself up, Mary. You know as well as I that I am telling you no falsehood. You might be able to fool others with your misguided attempts to be a great sorceress, but we both know you have no more power than this rock does. Now cease these lies once and for all."

"'Tis as I have said about his son, my lady. He took me over and over one day and I conceived his bastard. When I went to his father when he'd do nothing to support me, I was beaten again and brought before the group you found me with."

They also knew this to be only partly true. Michael had taken Mary, anywhere that he could find a hard surface. But she had enjoyed their coupling as much as he had. It wasn't until she was full of a child that she complained. That was when he'd hit her, knocked her away from him, and scorned the woman. After going to the man's father, she was taken into the cell that had held her until she was to be burned like nothing more than meat upon a spit. Anthony thought that humans, for the most part, were an odd group of beings.

Anthony wished that he could take all the men in the world that would raise their hand to someone smaller and without means of protecting themselves and burn them. It would take a lot of his flame, he thought...there were that many horrid people in the world. But there were times, he also knew, that the women could be just as mean, just as cruel as any man could be. Sometimes, in his experience, more so. People in general, he had learned, were not willing to think before speaking when they felt an injustice had been done to them.

"We have need of your help, in the form of a female child...your child. Her magic is greater than your own and will need guidance in the world that we live in. If you do not listen to me, follow my direction, she will surely die and you will be burned at the stake that we have saved you from this night." Mary rubbed her hand over the babe there but said nothing. "Anthony and I have a place for you to go. A place where you will be safe and kept from harm should you do as you are told. There will be help as well, for you and any children you should have after you have given us this help. You will have more than enough coin to keep you, and food enough to never feel the pangs of hunger again. All you have to do is keep the babe safe and help her grow into her magic.

If you wish to say no, then we will leave you to yourself and go about our business. But know this; you will die, soon, and by the flame that nearly licked at your feet this night, Mary Wayne."

"I have no wish to die, my lady. But I've no way of keeping her safe either, unless you do indeed help me. Even now he plots my death." Anthony knew this to be true, but also knew that his son was now dead, as cold as the ground that he fell upon. Not from the hand of the woman here, but because his own lady wife had found out about the babe Mary carried and the others. She had poisoned him. "I cannot keep myself safe now, much less a child. You say I will have coin? Servants? Someone to cook for me?"

"Yes. We shall protect you." Mary began shaking her head even as his lady wife spoke. "You know what we are, Mary. You have known this since you were a child at your own mother's feet. A dragon can protect you like none can. And we shall."

"My babe, she has meaning to you? You wish to buy her from me? I will gladly birth her and sell her to you." Eve shook her head; they would not lie to the woman, but they couldn't tell her why they'd not take her from her mother. They might not give her all the truths of it, but they'd not lie to her. "Then you take her. Raise her as your own so that she'll be safe, and I will live in this house you have given me for payment. With the servants, of course. I shan't be able to keep a house like I need on my own."

Anthony wanted to tell her no, that someone as selfish and greedy as her should be punished. To think that she'd sell her own flesh and blood for nothing more than a house.

Anthony would no more do that than he would cut off his lovely wife's head. He wished now that they'd never seen the future, especially the one in which they needed this woman's help.

"We cannot take your child. And should you wish not to do this, there will be no coin, no servants, and no home to keep you safe. You must do as we tell you. The hour grows late and the men are, as you said, plotting." He and Eve moved forward, deeper into the forest where the house was, knowing in their hearts that they'd have to convince this woman no matter what. But they also needed to be firm in their dealings with her. "You will come with us now. We will protect you and the babe so long as you do as you are told. We've set up this place to be safe and ready for you, with people there to help you once you have given birth."

It took them nearly an hour to get her settled in her new home. Anthony wanted to shift, show her how well they could protect as they said they would and be done with it all. But he knew that while she believed what they were, she would be terrified to see him. As they walked along to a safe place to shift, he spoke to his lady. Yes, they had done what they had come to do, but there were still going to be repercussions for young Mary Wayne.

"You have not told her the whole of her life. Nor have you told her she must love both her children equally. She will not, and you know this." Eve said that it would do her no good to do so. "Yes, but you know as well as I that she will misunderstand what we have put before her."

"Yes. And that will be good for the child too. The second

child will survive, not by her mother's hand, but because she will be left to her own devices. She will learn and survive as a strong woman. There are others there that will make sure that she gets what she needs to live and be what we need her to be. What all of us need for her to be." Anthony knew this as well. "I have managed to help the children, not once as we had planned, but with both the magical powers they will need. Especially the second born. Her immortality is set now; they both, provided that they are born, will live for a great many years."

"They will live then? Despite their mother's inability to see the clear picture?" She said they would. "My love, my life, I don't know if I can do this. To think.... I cannot lose you like this. We have so much to give. And our children, we shan't see them grow and become the men we hope for them to be."

"I know this too. And it grieves me so that I will never touch their skin, see them smile. We must do this, Anthony. You know this as well as I. Because if we don't do this, then all will be lost. As will our children." He nodded, his heart heavy with what they knew was coming. "Anthony, our children, do you think them to be great men? Men that will think of us when this all comes to pass?"

"They will love us no matter what we have done for them. This, this will ensure that our line does not end, but more importantly, that a great many lives will go on as well." She nodded and reached for his hand. Taking hers, he put his hand over her heart and told her that he loved her.

"And I you. And will beyond our deaths. You have been the reason for my heart beating, my blood pounding in my body since I first touched you." He wanted to stop now, take her into his arms and hold her. But he could not. Things were in motion now, things that they could see coming, and if they did not act now, everything and everyone would be lost.

Chapter 1

Kiaran sat very still. His body hurt; there wasn't a part of him that he thought had not been touched by the magic and power that he'd received from the witch. Erin, he knew, was dead. He looked at Asher when he joined him at the table; he too was feeling the effects of the power.

"Essie, she is all right?" Asher nodded, but said nothing to him. "I had no choice, Asher. I could feel her fear, taste it on my tongue. It was take it or no one would ever know who killed her. And in honesty, it wasn't that much magic, but the way that we received it is what hurt us so. I think I have the memories, but we all shared in the pain of receiving it."

"I know that. And I am also aware that you had no time to warn us. The magic, I can taste something on it that we have encountered before. She wasn't just a witch either. I felt wolf there as well." Kiaran nodded. His parents were the magic that Asher tasted, along with the wolf. He told him what he'd figured out and Asher didn't seem the least bit surprised by it. "Do you suppose that she was one of the others' mates? That she was to come here and help us?"

"I don't know. I honestly don't have any idea." Kiaran looked at Essie and stood when she came in the room. She was due soon; their child was going to be born before the next full moon. When she was seated, he poured her some tea and gave her a plate of the fresh scones that Grandda had made last evening. Christ, he loved this woman with all that he was. "We were just discussing Erin and her magic. And whether or not she might have been mate to one of our brothers."

"I was thinking the same thing. But did you see the darkness too?" Kiaran only nodded. Yes, he'd seen it, and had even tried to touch it. It wasn't magic, but hatred and cruelty. Erin had not been one that he would have liked to have encountered. "Would you say that she was a dark witch? Not like Helena was, but close?"

"Not close, no, but she did use the dark arts as her magic. I haven't any idea what she was to us, but my parents, they had a hand in her life. The darkness of her soul however, that is something that makes me think that perhaps she'd been cruel to others." Kiaran moved out of the way of Elbert when he entered the kitchen as his dog. "What do you suppose we're supposed to do with this magic and knowledge, other than to find her killer?"

"I've no idea."

Grandda changed then, his body becoming the man that he'd known his entire life, leaving behind the dog as if he were taking off a warm sweater. Kiaran knew that if anyone would know about the woman and her magic, he would, and asked him about it.

"I know not, but as the other witches are here, Caroline and Gobi, we could ask them." Grandda set a plate of food in front of Essie and took the scones. There was fruit as well as grain and fresh eggs. As she glared at him, he was all smiles at Essie when he returned his gaze to her. "You must eat better. These sweets will give you energy, but the babe, it needs this more."

As they talked about the day they had planned, the witch and all the million and one things that seemed to be on their plate at all times, Kiaran leaned back in his seat and thought about his family. They were all here and happy, and to him, that was enough. He thought also of becoming a father and what that would mean for them all. He only wished that his own parents were here to witness the birth of—

Hello. The touch to his mind had him looking at Essie and Asher. Neither one of them seemed to have been contacted, so he only waited. Whoever or whatever the person was, he wasn't going to show his hand just yet. *You don't know me. Well, that's obvious. But my sister, she had contact with you before.... She died, and I need to speak to you about who might have done it.*

I saw his face. I think she made sure of it. Kiaran could feel that while the person was magical, he felt no wolf about her. *You said you were her sister? How is that possible when she was a wolf and you aren't? I mean, I don't mean to be presumptuous, but I do know what she was.*

You have her memories, correct? Then I'm pretty sure you can figure out that she went by her own rules. Being a wolf, for whatever reason, suited her, and so she did it. I don't know what else to tell you. She found herself someone to convert her and there you go. Do they perhaps do it differently where you're from? Kiaran smiled. *Christ, can't you just think of the person who killed her and let me do my thing?*

And what thing might that be? Do you plan to kill him as well? The person said nothing. *My name is Kiaran. Maybe we should start with introductions.*

Or maybe we shouldn't. And yes, I plan to kill them all. He asked her what she meant. *You're not going to just let me have the information, are you? You're going to have to have it all or hound me until I have to come there, beat the shit out of you, and then get what I need. I mean the Herald. A group of idiots that have been around longer than.... Well, perhaps not longer than you, but I'd say it's close. Anyway, they killed her for what she is.*

A witch. The person didn't answer him, but then he really didn't need her to. Kiaran thought of the women with him and on a hunch, he decided to see what she might say. *Have you heard of Caroline? Perhaps Ariannona or Gobi?*

Yes. The voice, the fear in it, had him sitting up straighter in his seat. He looked at Asher when he said his name and asked for a moment. *Are they safe?*

Yes. As safe as we can make them. Are you a witch as well? No answer. *Perhaps it would be safer for you should you tell me your name and let me see if they know you.*

They do. Both of them do. He started to ask her which two when she continued. *Erin was my sister. Erin Wayne. If you speak to any of them, tell them that she is dead and that you have her memories. I won't contact you again unless I have to. I hope that I don't, but I might have no choice in the matter.*

24

It was almost as if they had been on a handheld phone, the snapping of the connection was that loud and that complete. Kiaran tried to reach out to her again, knowing that with the slight connection she'd used to contact him, he should be able to. But she had cut that avenue off as well. He told Asher and Essie what was said.

"You think she means them harm? The other witches, I mean?" Kiaran had no idea why, but he told Asher that he didn't think so. "You go and talk to them, tell me what they say, and I'll go on out to the castle. If you need me, just yell."

"I will. But I have a feeling that there is more to this than just what she told me. The Herald was indeed after Erin, but I'm betting from the memories, that she wasn't all that nice of a person to begin with. And I'm not so sure about the sister either." Asher just shook his head, as if resigning himself to this problem to solve as well. "I'll ask if I can see them today, this morning if possible."

Kiaran asked to meet the women. They had been staying on the land for the last few weeks, each of them doing their part to help out where they could. Even Gobi, who he'd found out that even though she was considered a *new* witch, she was nearly two hundred years old. Caroline...well, he'd not had the nerve to ask her about her age. He was pretty sure that he didn't want to know. Ariannona said she'd meet them there in a bit, she had to help Izic with a project he was having issues with.

He told the witches the same thing he had Asher, even about how she'd not told her what her name was.

"Erin Wayne? Yes.... I have to say, it's been a very long

time since I've heard the name. She was trouble from the beginning, and I try my best to avoid it when I can. Her mother…good heavens." Caroline got up and left them there, and returned seconds later with a book in her hand. To say she left them as in she simply went into another room would have been wrong…she simply left. "Mary Wayne was her mother. A little bitty thing, stupid as the day is long if I remember correctly. Anyway, yes, you're right, your parents did have a little to do with the magic that her children carry. Mary was one of many women that the Herald murdered when the group was first started. The Herald, named for the man who had started the group, was said to be a sadist and cared no more for his daughters than most men their dogs. Mayhap he treated the dogs better. He might well have not even known their names. But he was a man that would bend the Bible to suit his own needs or issues. His son, Michael, wasn't much better. He was a man that had more bastards than most men twice his age did. The father nearly as many. Mary was said to have carried the younger Herald's child, and it got her under the watchful eye of Rohm Herald. I think she was burned at the stake when the girls, her daughters, were nothing but teenagers. Erin was a willful child. Cruel at times and full of her own self. Her magic wasn't that great. And she and her mother practiced the dark arts more often than not. But this other child…? I have to admit, I don't know a great deal about her other than to tell you that she was born and that's all. Her name eludes me at the moment. But Erin, as I said, was a troublesome girl. Mary indulged her overly much and she turned out spoiled. Not too badly, but enough that most would rather smack her around than speak to her."

"When we got her magic and memories, we could feel that my parents had a little to do with it. We were wondering if you think she might have been a mate to one of the others." Caroline said that she had no idea but doubted it. "I didn't think so either. But it was worth a shot. This other girl though, she's not wolf."

"What do you mean? Neither of them.... Are you sure you have the right magic? What a silly question, of course you do. But wolf? Not sure. I suppose she could have found someone to turn her, but I've not been privy to it." Caroline thumbed through some of her pages and turned it to him. "You should read this. I meant to show you sooner, but we've been getting settled and all. And Gobi and I have been working on a few spells to keep us all safer."

He was still reading when Ariannona joined them. Izic wasn't with her, but she looked frazzled and a little angry. Kiaran started to ask her what was going on when she put her hand up. He grinned, thinking that for someone so tiny, Izic could get into more trouble than most full grown adults.

"He's got him a mate, as you know." Kiaran nodded. This was going to be epic, he knew it. "Well, now he wants a house. Not a house for a brownie, but one the size of mine. He wishes to fill it with children with his good wife."

"That's a lot of children." She nodded, still pissy. "So what did you tell him? I'm assuming that didn't go over well."

"You have no idea. When I asked him about how many children he thought that might be, reminding him that he couldn't sire children on his own, he told me that his lady wife would be finding them and bringing them to their home.

27

Sort of like an orphanage. When I looked at her to see if she was in on this…whatever it was, she was looking at Izic like he'd lost his mind. I bet you a nickel that she had no idea what was going on until that moment." Kiaran laughed and Ariannona turned to him. "He thought—and I kid you not—he thought that should the house be filled with children that the queen would bless him with a title. Just any old title, he told me. But he thought he'd like one, especially after all he'd done. And don't get me started on his list. It's as ridiculous as this idea of his."

"I see." Kiaran was having a hard time not bursting out laughing. Ariannona could and would hurt him if she didn't see the humor in this. "And did you talk to Essie? What sort of title is she going to find for him?"

"She won't be giving him my suggestion, that's for sure." He asked her what that might have been. "Lord of the Fools and Court Jester of Idiots among others. But she said that it was too much of a mouthful. I then suggested that we just knock him around a bit, and you know how she can get. So I guess that's not an option."

Kiaran couldn't help it, he did laugh, and nearly fell to the floor with it. Every time he looked at Ariannona, he could see Essie putting a crown of little bells on the brownie's head, and his toes would be covered in long curled shoes. Every step Izic would take, he'd sound like an ice cream truck coming to feed his several million children.

"This is not funny." And that, of course, sent him into more peals of laughter. He had not had this much fun in a very long time. "He's going to want a scepter after this as well."

Kiaran left the room. It was that or he was going to get himself killed by his sister-in-law. Taking the book with him, knowing that he couldn't leave the house with it because of the magic protecting it, he went into the large living room and sat on the couch. Spurts of laughter still spilled from his lips, but he soon got deeper into the story that Caroline had asked him to read.

~~~

Lelani wasn't sure what she was supposed to do now. Her sister, she knew, was dead, but how or by whom wasn't going to come to her. She had no one left now, not a single uncle or aunt, no one. Not that she'd had all that much contact with her sister in the first place, but it was the point of the thing.

Feeling sorry for herself wasn't going to get her work done, so she leaned over the tapestry and tried to see where the stitching started to change colors. It was difficult, not only because the person who had brought it to her to look at was hanging right over her shoulder, but the rug stank, like someone had taken a major dump on it and had not cleaned it. When she sat up again, stretching her neck muscles, Lelani knocked heads with the man.

"You didn't warn me again. You have to warn me when you're going to sit up so that this doesn't happen." She really didn't think she should have to warn him when she was needing a break. "Don't you think this would go faster if you'd just keep working on it? I mean, every hour you have to get up and move. That's not very productive of you if you ask me. I don't care how long this takes, I just think that you're wasting time by not working on it very hard."

"I didn't ask you. And I told you this was going to take some time. More time than I can do at a continuous pace." She stood up then and he glared at her. "Mr. Winer, why don't you just go away? Christ, you're driving me insane with your constant harping and whining."

Lelani wasn't nice, she knew this. Nor was she overly sympathetic to people. In fact, she didn't care for them at all. She liked to be alone. People, for the most part, were noisy, manipulative, as well as a pain in the ass most of the time.

"I told you when I brought this here that I was going to keep an eye on you in the event you tried to do something to my prize, and claim that it was in a worse condition than it had been before I brought it to you. This means a great deal to me." She glanced at the tapestry, then back at him. "I want it repaired and cleaned today. So you should get to work on it. You're not doing as you were told."

"And I told you, several times as a matter of fact, that I don't work that way. You want it cleaned quickly, I suggest you take it to the local laundromat and have them do it. Otherwise, as I told you, it will be several weeks before I can repair it, then several more before it's cleaned. And as far as claiming it was in worst shape than when you brought it in, well, that's not going to be possible. Have you smelled this thing? Someone hasn't taken care of it." He lifted his finger up, and if he poked her with it again, she was going to snap it off at the joint. Taking a step back from him, she came to a decision. "I think we're done here. It's time you left. Take your piece of shit tapestry and get out of my shop."

"You'll be done when I say we're done. And not a moment

before." She only looked at him. Surely he wasn't going to try and make her clean this thing, was he? "You'll get your ass back to it now. And no more breaks either, Erin. I'm not paying you to lollygag around like this. And when my friends get here, we'll all have a nice little talk about things."

"I see." She moved to the rug again, but this time she rolled it up instead of leaning over it. When she handed it over to him, he stepped back, crossed his arms over his chest, and told her he wasn't taking it. Honestly, she was a little afraid. He thought her to be her sister. He was from the Herald. "Well then, I'm going to toss it out of my shop and you'll have to deal with it out there. And if you give me any more shit, you'll be on the sidewalk with it."

"You will not talk to me this way. Nor will you be throwing our merchandise out on the ground. If you're not going to work, then you can sit your ass down and wait." She asked him who he was waiting for. "You'll see when they get here. We've been following you and your deeds for a very long time."

"Good for you." Reaching for the phone when he didn't take the rug again, she dialed Roger; the man, for lack of a better term, was everything to her. He was so much more than just her friend; he was her only friend actually, as well as her familiar. When he answered, she knew that he was going to give her a hard time about using the phone to talk to him. Lelani cut him off before he could make her laugh. "Hey, can you come down here? I have an issue." He told her he'd be right down and she set the phone back in the cradle.

"And this person you called. You think to have him make

me leave here before I'm finished with my assignment? I have news for you, it won't work, Erin. You and he both are in for a major disappointment. I have people coming that are going to show you the error of your ways." Lelani had had enough. Reaching into the man's head, she raped it until his ears and nose were bleeding. Finding what she wanted, she dropped the rug on the floor and stepped back from him. Christ, she was right. He was there to kill her. "Find it, Erin? Do you know who I am, what I want?"

His laughter made her skin crawl as he wiped at the blood that was now on his chin. She'd not been gentle with getting the information that she needed, and he was paying the price for it. When he drew a gun from the back of his pants, she stood still, pulling some magic around her before he hurt her. Or he tried to hurt her. Lelani was a good deal stronger than her sister had been, and smarter. But she wasn't taking any chances with this extremist.

"I'm not Erin. You've got the wrong girl. My sister is dead." He laughed again, and this time she could hear the insanity in his voice. Reaching out to Roger to warn him, the gun went off just as she was gathering more magic from around the room to protect both herself and Roger. As soon as the man dropped, his neck broken by Roger when he'd grabbed him, she sat down as well. That had been a mistake she'd not make again. Her ribs were aching from the impact of the bullet, though it had not pierced her skin.

"You okay?" She nodded and Roger told her to look at him. "You've been hurt. Again. I told you to put some of that magic around here. You have to listen to me, girl."

"I just wanted to be normal." He told her that ship done

sank a few centuries ago. "Erin, he was here for Erin. They're still after her, even now. I never felt that when he arrived. I knew he was armed but not why he was here, other than the tapestry. I should have checked, but I wanted him to be just a man needing work from my shop."

"They've been practicing to keep you from finding out, I guess. Using some of the magic that they profess to hate so much. I'm betting that they got someone to help them, because Erin could feel what their intent was. But she's gone now, and I thought them to be done with this foolishness. Mayhap they'll quit as soon as the paper comes out. Don't you think?" Roger reached down and picked up the man one handed. "I'll take care of this one, and you clean up in here when I'm gone. And not before. You know I might leave droppings."

Droppings. He meant blood or something else that might lead whoever came for her instead of her sister back to them. If they didn't know where she was already. Lelani should have known that things had been too quiet for her for too long. Again, she had so much to thank her sister for.

When she heard the door to the back of her shop open and then close, Lelani closed her eyes and swept the room. Not with a broom, though the place could have used a good sweep, but with her magic, covering up every detail of the place that had been hers so that no one would find the man had been murdered here. Her tools were cleaned, the blood from the man's nose gone as well. No fingerprints or shoe marks. There was no hair in the seldom used broom, no trash in the wastepaper baskets.

Then for a little extra, she did clean up the place. Dusting and sweeping had not been her cup of tea and the place looked it. When Roger returned, he looked around but said nothing. He'd been after her for a week now to at least let him dust the room's only furniture other than her table.

"I have to move again. We can no longer stay here if they are still looking for her. And that man, the one that has her magic, they might follow that to him. I'm not sure how but they might. They did track me down, and I haven't had a thing to do with Erin in decades." Roger said he was ready. "You don't have to come with me anymore, Roger. I think I can take care of myself. Usually. You must want to have a life of your own."

"I made a promise. I'm aiming to keep it. Besides, who would you have cooking for you? You know you can't boil water without causing a fire." She pointed out that it had happened over three hundred years ago. "A man never forgets when his hair is on fire and his manhood is about to be taken out with flames."

"It wasn't that bad." He only cocked his head at her. "Okay, it did take down that house and the one next to it, but I've been really careful since then. And the only reason that your manhood was in jeopardy was because you were sleeping in the hall when I came toward the door with the flaming grease. Had you been in a bed then I wouldn't have fallen and the fire wouldn't have hit so close to you."

"You should not have been making yourself something to eat in the middle of the night with the flames so high on the fire. And you have been careful. The last time you caused a fire, let me see, there was only the stove that time. Oh, and the pot. Plus, there was the—"

"Enough. You've made your point." She really didn't want to leave him anyway. "I have to make arrangements here and close this place up. Money isn't a problem, but we might want to think about a new car this time. The one we have now, it's a little out of date."

He told her it was a great deal out of date. As he looked around, making sure there was nothing left behind, she thought of their mode of transportation and smiled.

It was very old, and it was also a large hearse, complete with velvet curtains and a large door in the back that opened to put caskets in and take them out. When he'd gotten it, there had been a casket in the back, and it had taken her nearly ten years to convince him to get it out of there. It had been drawing unwanted attention. To this day he still spoke of how much fun it was at the grocery store when people walked by it.

"I'll find us something fun this time. How about something compact?" She just looked at him. Compact with a man his size would mean that only one of them would be inside. "Have I told you lately that I care not for your looks when you deem to spear me with them? Besides, I could be my animal. That would save us lots of room."

"Yes, you could do that if you wish. But I was thinking, and this is just a thought, that if someone would see me driving down the road with a wild animal, a lynx, in the car with me, that might draw more attention than your casket did. But besides that, I think we should go find this person Erin gave her magic to. I need to make sure that he's safe. She never cared about others and how they were affected when she did something. I, however, need to make sure that the Herald doesn't find out about him because of her." He nodded, but she could tell that he wasn't so sure about this. Neither was she, really. "He might be hurting from it as well. I mean, he's old, yes, but she might have hurt him in some way. Right?"

"She could have. You thinking that she might have left you some of herself in him? A memory or two for you?" She hoped so...not for her, but if he'd let her go through Erin's memories she might be able to figure out why her sister had hated her so much. "Lelani, if you go there, you do know that you won't like what you find. I understand having to do this, but it might be better left unsaid. Your sister, she wasn't a nice person."

"Yes, I'm aware of that. But I need to know. I just.... I need to know." He nodded and told her that he'd find a nice vehicle to use. Something big enough to carry him and whatever she wanted to take with them. There was no need for it really, but she did have a few things that were her treasures, and she'd never part with them. "Roger? Thank you for being my only friend."

"You know as well as I that we have more than friendship, Lelani. We are one, you and I." He was right, Roger had long since ceased being her friend, and was now all she had in this whole wide world. They had gone well beyond just being buddies. Roger, as her animal to call, was all they needed in each other.

By the time she had cleaned out the building, including the upper and lower levels, no one would ever find a trace of either of them there. Just like in her workstation, not a single hair or a print would be found should anyone go looking. Nor hers or Roger's name on anything attached to it in rent due or outstanding bills. Not even the dead man that had lost his life there. The building was as clean as any lab at any police station, maybe even cleaner. And when they left the area, driving out of the little burg like she had always preferred when finding a home, not a single person would remember their faces either. It was just the way they needed it to be. Lelani Wayne and Roger did not exist as far as anyone knew.

"How you gonna do this, Lelani? You gonna be your usual self, or are you gonna try and be nice?" There was no point in trying to deny that she wasn't ever nice. But she did tell him where they were headed. "Ohio again, huh? Is she there? Either of them other witches, you think them to be there too?"

"Yes, they both are, I think. Even Gobi; I don't know her, but I have heard of her. That man, he said that both Caroline and Ariannona were there and safe." He nodded and started the large pickup that he'd gotten them. "He said his name was Kiaran, the one that Erin gave her memories and magic to. There is something else as well. He's a dragon, a very old one at that."

He nearly drove them into a large semi, she'd startled him so badly. When he asked her if she was nuts, Lelani told him that honestly she had no idea. But this was something that she needed to do. While he was lost in the art of driving—as he called it—Lelani thought of the stories she'd heard as a child, of the great dragon couple that had saved her mother. Fat lot of good it had done them. Her mom had been killed by the very people that had tried before they had been born, and Lelani had come to hate even the very mention of the royal couples'

37

names. Not that she blamed them for her mother's death...
that was on her mother. But hearing about how wonderful
they were, how they had picked her mother over hundreds of
other witches, had gotten on her last nerve. Anthony and Eve
had been nothing to her. Erin and her mother had had it all.

By the time they decided to rest for the night, they had
covered half the distance to the man that might or might not
have answers for her. She thought about contacting him again,
to tell him that she was coming, but it was well after midnight.
Crawling into bed, Roger as his cat beside her, she thought of
the man Kiaran and wondered if he was any relationship to
the king and queen. It would be her luck that he'd be their
great, so many times removed grandchild, and that he'd look
just like the king. Not that she knew what the king had looked
like, but she'd heard stories of his handsomeness from her
mother, over and over, until she had avoided any mention of
the man or his equally lovely wife.

Chapter 2

Shane was putting the last piece into place on his wall when he saw Essie. She was coming across the field with a picnic basket when he saw the stranger walking toward Essie. It took him only a moment to jump down to the earth and make his way to Essie. Whoever this person was, she could not have ill intent in her heart or she'd not be on the land, but he didn't know her. When she reached Essie before he did, Shane felt fear. Moving quicker now, he was joined by Asher and Kiaran, and they too looked afraid. The woman turned to them just as they were nearly to her.

"She's in labor." The stranger's voice was strong and clear. Shane looked around, thinking that Lindsey was there as well. "Her, you dolt. She's having this baby now. Why the hell are you making her tote your lunch out here when she needs to be resting?"

As soon as Asher picked Essie up in his arms, she screamed. When he stopped, even breathing, Shane thought, Asher looked at him. There wasn't just fear there, but he thought his brother looked ill as well. He could not imagine the total fear that was reflected on Asher's face. The woman snapping her fingers in front of their faces had them looking at her.

"Lay her down here." Nodding, Asher did as the woman said. "Send the dragon to the house. We'll need blankets and some string. Do you have a good knife?"

No one moved. When she stood up and slapped Asher across the face, he put his hand to his cheek and stared at her. Shane took a step back, knowing that Asher was going to kill her for doing something so unprovoked.

"Are you here? You've not gone off again, have you?" Asher nodded then shook his head, his hand still on his face. "Good, you're at least thinking how to nod. This is going to be fine. Have the dragon go to the house and get blankets, string, and a sharp knife. Stay with me and I'll not have to harm you again, do you understand me?"

"Yes. But Essie, she's my wife." The woman said nothing but turned back to Essie, who was laying on the dirt, her body tight in pain. "I want to stay with her. She's our wife."

"Well good for you. But if you want this baby brought into his world before she's college ready, then I suggest we work together. And try not to zone out on me again." Asher looked at Keion, who had just joined them. After being told what was needed, he left them. Asher went to the ground on his knees when Kiaran did. "She's in the final stages. Do you know what that means?"

"Yes. She's ready to give birth. But I thought there would be time. A slow movement through labor and then delivery. Shouldn't we wait to see if that happens?" The woman asked Essie, politely, to put her knees up. Shane moved back when it was apparent the baby was coming now, just as the stranger said. Asher and Kiaran moved to either side of her, each of them taking her hands. "What can we do?"

"I'm pretty sure that you've done about all you can about bringing this babe into the world by planting it there. What I want you to do now is keep her calm. She gets any tenser and we'll never get this baby out." Asher said he could do that. When the woman turned to Shane, all he could think about was her beauty. When she hit him in the belly, he focused on what she was telling him. "Are you stupid? Christ, I'm working with a yard full of idiots. I said go get some bottled water. The ones that might be warmed by being in the sun. Hurry."

He was away and getting as many as he could carry when he realized that she was bossing them around like she was in charge. Shane figured that in this, she could be. Actually, he was glad someone was taking over for them, as none of them seemed to have a clue as to what they were doing. He did wonder where Grandda was. He'd been the one that said he'd deliver the child for Kiaran and Asher.

In only a few moments, Essie was screaming. It didn't seem to be from pain, though he was sure she was, but more like she was grabbing up energy by doing it. Christ, he was sure that nary an animal would return to the forest for months, if not years, after hearing her letting herself go like

41

that. But when Keion returned with a large bag in his claws, Shane started emptying out whatever was in it and handing it to the woman.

"Knife, or scissors, if you can find any." He handed her a pair of scissors that had been buried at the bottom. When she took them, Shane didn't look how she was utilizing them as he separated out the other items so that they'd be able to grab them should she need them. For some reason, he didn't want to make her any pissier than she seemed to be right now.

The sound of a baby crying had him looking at Essie. She was holding this little bundle in her hands and sobbing. Asher, too, was crying, and Kiaran looked as if he'd been hit, hard and repeatedly. When Essie pulled the blanket down, he got his first look at the little girl. Christ, she was more beautiful than her mother, which he'd not thought at all possible.

Handing the woman whatever she needed without thinking about it, he helped her with Essie. It was messier than he'd thought it would be, this birthing thing. But he wouldn't have missed this for the world. His first niece, the first baby that had been born to their family in centuries, was here, and mother and daughter seemed to be just fine. Thanks, he knew, to this stranger.

When the woman stood up, he did as well. She watched Asher and Kiaran as they fussed with Essie and their daughter. "Can someone take her home? There is no reason that she needs to be out here anymore, but keep her warm and lying down for a few more days. She will need plenty of that, and food. Also juice. I'm sure with witches around, you have plenty of that."

"We do and I will. You'll come along too, yes?" She shook

her head at Asher and told him she'd only been coming to see someone. "Perhaps I can help you find them. It's the very least we can do for what you've done for me this day. My name is Asher. This is my wife, Essie, and our partner, Kiaran. You would be?"

"Kiaran?" When Kiaran nodded she took a step back from them all. "You're a dragon? You're the man that my sister sent her life force to? I didn't.... The magic here is very strong; I'm assuming that is why I didn't feel you when I felt the babe call to me. I just assumed that you'd be human."

"Yes, we like to keep others from figuring out who and what we are. You must be Lelani. I know your name because we've been looking into your life. My parents, Anthony and Eve, I believe you might have had some dealings with them. Or your mother would have. They protected you and your family." She shook her head and Shane moved up behind her. The need to protect her, to help her, made him feel the need to tell Kiaran to leave her alone. "You don't believe me?"

"Oh, I'm sure you were told all sorts of things they might have done for my sister and mother. They were safe, well cared for, and even taken care of after news was brought to us that the king and queen had been murdered. Even after my own mother was brutally murdered, they continued on as if nothing changed. I suppose that for Erin, it didn't. But I was never a part of that good fortune. My sister was the firstborn, and thusly I was not as important nor a part of the magic that came to them, according to my mother. But that has nothing to do with why I'm here. I only want to see the memories you got from my sister so that I can figure something out." Kiaran looked at Shane, then at Lelani again as she continued. "But I have a feeling that it's not going to be simple, is it? Well fuck. I guess I've made a mistake coming here. I'm glad that your child is well and so is your wife, but I'm going to leave now, and I'd rather not have to hurt you so that you don't follow."

"No, please don't go. I'd very much like to talk to you about what you've been led to believe. I have no idea how to give you a look into her memories, but as you have helped bring my daughter into this world safely, I'll let you have what you wish. But I would also like a chance to ask you why you think you were not a part of the protection my parents put out there for you." Lelani said nothing. "Will you stay? At least until we can get Essie settled?"

"For a little while, but I have a friend. If he isn't welcome, then no, I can't stay." Asher said he was welcome as well as he moved toward their home. Shane moved with them, his hands itching to touch Lelani. When he felt the touch of his other half, he smiled at his humor when he asked if he thought she was always so friendly. But Lelani asked Asher after her friend again. "He's magical and only answers to me. Is that a problem?"

"No. I don't believe it will be. So long as he doesn't hurt anyone here or create any issues, then things will be fine between us. But I don't think he will do either, will he?" Lelani shook her head but said nothing to Asher. "Well, then you both are welcome to stay for as long as you wish."

You think that she is our mate? That stopped Shane. He looked around for Keion and told him that wasn't funny. *No, it's not, but you have been wanting to touch her for many moments. It's either that or she's naked. Naked women give you the same desires. Have you stripped her down without my knowledge, Shane?*

He felt Keion's humor and wanted to hunt him down and strangle him. *No. She's not naked. What a thing to suggest.* But it was planted there now, the thought of her naked. *Keion, you should come here. Now, if you please, as a man. I'd like to see what she might be to us.*

I was kidding. There was a slight panicked sound to his voice now, and Shane didn't blame him. *I have no desire to see a woman now that might or might not be our mate. I'm busy.*

But the thought of her as their mate did have merit. To have someone in their life, like his brothers did, would be amazing. And to know that she'd be there with them forever made his step a little lighter. All these thoughts, and he'd only just met her.

And you think that being busy will make a difference? It won't, in the event you were hoping so. Come to the house. I'd like to test this theory of yours. Keion said he'd come when he was finished with the stones he was moving to the castle grounds. There were so few left to move. *I think it can wait for one more day. Come here please. The sooner we get this sorted out for us, the sooner we can go back to our lives. Perhaps with her in it.*

Shane wasn't sure they'd ever have normal again. Not with all this other stuff going around. And now a mate to put in the mixture? Well, he wouldn't know for sure until he was able to touch her. While he was pretty sure she was, he wasn't going to jump the gun just yet. But Christ, she was beautiful.

When Essie was settled in her bed, Simeon went to find their grandda. No one had been able to contact him nor their dad since they'd found out about Essie, and they were worried. But almost as soon as he left the big bedroom that Essie had been put in, he returned with not just Grandda, but their father as well. He was told about the newest addition to the family.

"Well, it's a grand day for us all. Grand day. Lindsey went into labor just today as well, and had her own little bundle not an hour ago. That was where we were, bringing my granddaughter into the world. Little Eve Marie is as pretty as her momma. And I'm thinking that little Sally Anne here is just as.... Thank you for naming her for my dear love. She'd be so wonderfully happy." Grandda huffed at him and Dad smiled. "Are you saying I didn't help you? I was helpful; I did just what you told me to do when you told me to do it."

"You were no such thing. More in the way than the boys were underfoot when they were but babes themselves." Grandda handed Essie some broth and crackers. "You keep this down, love, and I will fix you a nice steak for dinner with all the trimmings. To think, two new babes in the household again."

As they fussed around with both the new babies, going back and forth between the two bedrooms, and his dad finally got to hold Sally Anne, Shane watched Lelani. She wanted to bolt, and she wasn't making any bones about it. Every time someone asked her if she needed anything, food or just a glass of juice, she told them that she'd not be there long and wouldn't want to waste anyone's time. Finally, when a cat, a lynx he thought it was, showed up, she settled, but not by much. The cat, Shane saw, was very protective of her. It was then that it occurred to him that he was the holder of some of her magic.

Familiar, he knew the term. Even Caroline had one…a bird that hung around her and did things. He was pretty sure that Gobi had taken one of the little faeries for her own as well. After Mystic, the girl who had worked for her, left, she said that she needed someone to talk to. Shane watched the cat and wondered again if this woman was his mate. He also knew that he'd have to get by the big guy in order to figure it out.

~~~

Lelani tried not to feel overwhelmed by all of them, but nothing she did was dissipating the panic that she was feeling. And the longer she stayed in the room with them, the higher her stress level got. There were more people in this one house than she'd seen in a month of Sundays in her own home. Trying her best to stay out of their way and not demand that she get to the memories, she leaned back in the chair and tried to relax.

You are going to be fine. She told Roger that she was not. They were breathing on her. *I don't believe they are doing any such thing. You're exaggerating again. No one is even near enough to you to touch. Breathing requires them to be at least nose distance. Why must you say things like that when you know them to not be true?*

Have I told you lately that I dislike you very much? He laughed at her and she reached to touch his head. *I shouldn't have come here. I knew it when we left. This is not a place that is going to welcome me any more than the mall does. He is fine, I knew that even then, and this family can protect itself better than I can.*

There you go again. How can an establishment not be

47

welcoming? By their very nature, they are supposed to make you feel as if you need to enter. They nearly lay down to welcome you into their establishment. Lelani told him to hush. *You know what I say is true. But you must tell me, why does that man stare at you as if you are an all-day sucker and he has to have a lick?*

Apt description. He laughed with her, then stiffened, his fur on end as he stood up. *What is it? What do you feel? Roger, what is it?*

Dragon. She wanted to tell him that there were several in the room with them, but she felt it too. Standing up to stand beside him, the fur on his body stiff with so many emotions that she didn't know which one to grasp, she drew magic around her and waited. The man standing in front of her suddenly startled her to whimper.

"Don't hurt him." She nodded, not sure how he knew what she'd been about to do, but watched him. "His name is Silco. He and his mate, Yviene, have come to pay homage to the new princess. Take the magic down and I'll let you go."

He'd been touching her; his hands weren't gripping her hard, but they held her firmly. When she backed from him, thinking to fall into the chair, her body was pressed tightly against another one behind her. Another male, this one a dragon. She didn't turn to him, but stood as still as she could when they both stepped closer, enclosing her between them and their heat. Her heart began beating so hard that she was sure they could feel it; they were that close. And when she put up her hands to push them away, he grabbed her hands in his and held them to his chest.

"Is she? Keion, is it her?" The man behind her might have answered the one in front of her, but she had no clue. When hands touched her again, rubbing her arms, her back, it was all she could do not to beg them to touch her more, to touch her in places they were missing. "My name is Shane Benson. The man behind you is Keion, my other half. A dragon."

"I know what he is. I need to breathe. Back up." Neither of them moved, but she tried again. "Please, you're too close. I'm not used to people touching me, standing this close to me. It's too much right now. I like to be alone."

"You're our mate. I'm sure you know what that means." She nodded, then shook her head. "I see. About the way I feel right now. I want you in my life, in our lives, but we're not sure what to do to make you feel welcome."

"You can start by letting me go. I only came to see why my sister hated me so much." They didn't move, not that she thought they would, but she was starting to panic, her body burning to be free. She felt trapped, buried alive and drowning all at the same time. "You have to back up. I can't... you're too close."

Roger was there, snarling at them, but she was beginning to panic; a meltdown was coming. Tearing from both men, she ran through the big house and to the front door. She made her way to the yard and fell to the ground, even as her magic overpowered her. She wasn't able to hold onto it any longer, and when she released it, not if but when, there was going to be trouble.

"Breathe." Lelani jerked from the woman who grabbed her chin. "I said to breathe. In your nose and out of your mouth. Do it damn it, before I have to knock you out to help you control it."

"I can't." The woman said that she could and she would. Lelani tried to breathe, bringing in the air that smelled of the two men. Closing her eyes, she tried to level out, to make things better, but the woman laughed. "This isn't fucking funny."

"It is from where I am. Keep breathing, and I might not have to get myself hurt by knocking you on your ass. You should have more control over yourself. You're too old to be like this. What happened in there that put you to this point? Did those two say something to you? Did they hurt you?" Lelani told her to fuck off. "Yes, that's good. Focus yourself on anger and not on whatever it is that took you under."

As her breathing leveled out, so did her heartrate. She was still stressed by it all…the men, the crowd, her sister. It was too much in too little time. Lelani looked up at the woman she'd seen in the house with one of the other men. A witch. A strong one, but a witch all the same.

"There are too many of them. I'm not used to being around so…well, anyone but Roger. It was just too much." The woman said something like there are more, but Lelani thought she might not want to know for sure. "This was a mistake. I shouldn't have come here."

"I doubt that. But I would like to thank you for bringing Essie's baby into the world. The rest of us were with Lindsey and we hadn't any idea. It's my fault that they couldn't get in touch with us. We were so focused on her that I sort of shut out the rest of the world for a little while. But I'm to understand that you got it done, and without killing anyone too." Lelani sat down now and so did the woman. "Ariannona Benson; my mates are Elam and Casdon. You'd be Lelani Wayne. And

50

from the way that Shane was acting, I'd say you're his and Keion's mate."

"No, I'm sure you're all mistaken. Maybe my sister might have been, but not me. I'm not the sort that people mate with."

Ariannona asked her why not. But before she could come up with a reason, even one that made sense to her, Roger came and sat beside her. Rubbing her fingers through his fur, she felt herself calm down more by just having him close. She looked at the beautiful woman who was leaning back on her hands regarding her. When she smiled, Lelani had a feeling that things were not going to be as easy as she had hoped.

"I remember you. Not you really, but your family. Your mom, if you don't mind me saying so, was a flake." Lelani didn't say anything. It was the truth, so why try to make her out to be something that she wasn't? "I also remember your sister, Erin. I often wondered why the king and queen had given her what they had, but then today, after meeting you, I think I understand what they did. You're not a thing like her, are you? Thank goodness."

"What is it you think you understand?" When Roger stiffened, she looked to where he was looking. The men, all of them, were standing on the porch and staring at her. "My mother and sister lived near here. Not close, but within walking distance. I lived there as well, but not for long. I think I was about ten when I sort of gravitated out on my own. I knew about the Bensons as well. Never saw them; I don't think I was ever.... My mother and sister saw them when they were younger. They would often come to the edge of the property here to get a look at them. They'd actually pack a luncheon to bring to sit here and watch them. Kind of creepy if you ask me, but then that was my mom. That's what got her killed, not doing as she was supposed to, as she'd been warned to do. She was to stay where she was supposed to so that the magic would keep her safe."

"She was burned at the stake when you were about...I would say about thirteen or so, right?" Lelani nodded and looked at the other woman. "You were the one that they gave the most magic to...you are aware of that, aren't you?"

"Yes. After a time I was able to figure it out. I didn't understand it then, and still don't to this day. But I knew that was what had happened. It was a mistake that my family never let me forget. Erin was the firstborn, she should have had it all, not part of it. I don't think they knew about me, the king and queen anyway. At least that's what my mother always thought. I think.... I think that is why she never cared for me. I was a mistake, and the king and queen would never have approved of my living and taking from my sister. Not that either of them were all that willing to give anything easily, but I survived, I guess." Ariannona said nothing, but did look sad. It was the one thing that Lelani hated more than someone being fake...someone feeling sorry for her. Standing, she decided that it wasn't worth finding out about her sister's hatred for her. "I should be going. As I said, this was a mistake."

Ariannona didn't move but did look up at her. There was that smile again, sort of a cross between I know something you don't and you're in deep shit. It was a feeling that she'd had for the greater part of her life. And the main reason she was alone a great deal.

"You have a mark, don't you? A dragon on some part of your body that you have tried to hide all your life." Lelani looked at the man on the deck, Shane he'd said his name was, then back at the witch. "And the closer you got to here, the larger it got…might even be in color now. Mine is. And so is Keion's. I would imagine that when they touched you, the two of them up there, things in your body started to go a little nuts. Right?"

"Yes, but I have no idea what it means if you're going to ask me. I thought that it was there as a spell. A protection spell that the king and queen gave me that was meant for me to have because Erin was to get the magic. She wasn't marked that I know of. I'm sure that had she been, then my mom would have crowed about that as well. I think something happened and I messed with their plans, whatever those might have been. As I said, I was a mistake." Shane stood up now, having been seated on the steps. As he made his way to her, she backed up. Keion moved toward her with him, and she felt her body tense up again. But she felt it was important that the witch knew what she felt. "Erin and I didn't see each other a lot over the last few hundred years. I heard about her, but didn't have a lot of contact; not that she would have allowed it. She would tell anyone she knew that she had been chosen by the royal family. Chosen as what? Who knows? I'm pretty sure that's what got her into trouble. That and her inability to stay low."

Keion was standing with them now. Ariannona had stood up as well. They looked like friends, she supposed, embarking on some adventure together to have some fun. But they were anything but that; she wasn't even sure that she liked them yet. Lelani didn't have any friends. She'd been without them for too long to know how to have fun with these people.

"She didn't have one. A mark, I mean." Now Lelani looked at Kiaran when he spoke. "She sent me her thoughts, memories, and magic, so I know just about every detail of her life. She had a little magic, so you know. Not nearly as much as you, but there was no mark on her. Not from my parents at least. She'd had a tat put on when she was about fourteen, but it was painful for her so it was never finished. But she knew about yours. Her tattoo would have been pretty, colorful, and well done, but it wasn't put on her by magic, and she certainly didn't have the power that you have, as I said. I think, as do the rest of us, that you were meant to have it all."

"No, I wasn't born first." The other man, Essie's mate and holder of the dragon, Asher, asked her what that had to do with it. "You're king, king of the dragons, right? And the firstborn. Do you suppose that you're king simply because you're stronger? Braver? Or that simply because, as I said, you're firstborn?"

Asher, clearly embarrassed, said he had no idea how that would have worked had he been second or last, but it did. He nodded to the others, Kiaran and Ariannona, and they all three moved away from her. She nearly turned to leave, thinking that she'd had enough, when she was boxed in again. She found that Roger, too, had left her when she looked for him to help her. Her mates; she knew as well as they did what she was to them.

Shane was standing too close again, and so was his other half. She knew what they were, how they were one person when need be. It was all her mother had spoken of when she'd come back from her trips to see them. When Keion touched his fingers to her arm, Lelani felt her sigil burn, not painfully, but like it needed to be touched. Like all of her needed to be touched.

"Do you have any idea how long we've waited for you? How we've thought of you coming to us? Since the others have gotten their mates, it's been all we've talked about. It was scary, I will admit that much to you, but we were excited as well." Keion moved closer, and Shane, now at her back, was touching her as well. Keion touched his mouth to her throat as he continued. "The two of us, we'll take very good care of you if you'll let us. You will, won't you, Lelani? We'll share you too, with each other, whenever you'll have us."

"I don't want you, either of you." Even to her own ears, it sounded breathless, like whatever words spilled from her mouth were in direct contrast to how she really felt. "I'm not what you think I am. I'm rude and mean. I don't like people, and I hate being confined. You're touching me again."

"We are. I think you're enjoying it too, aren't you? How do you feel with us touching you? Overheated? I am...hard. I bet that your nipples are as hard as stones right now." She felt wonderful, like she was being pressed between two very warm blankets. But they were missing the point. She wasn't their mate. When Shane rocked into her ass she wanted to moan, and only just caught herself from doing so. "Can you feel how hard I am to take you? To lay you out on our bed and feast on every part of you? I can smell you."

"Don't do this." But she had a feeling it was much too late

for that now. When one of them picked her up—she wasn't sure who because they were both touching her, tugging and pulling at her clothing—she felt the cock between her legs, the hands at her breasts. And when Keion—she knew it was him because of the heat billowing off him—when he kissed her neck, then her breast, she came.

It was a short powerful punch to her system, nothing at all like she'd ever felt before during sex. It was as if they were teaching her things, making her feel…well, feel everything. Lelani felt it everywhere…her head, her eyes, even her toes seemed to have been touched by it. But it wasn't enough. Need clawed at her, made her hurt with it, and she started pulling at their clothing too.

The softness of the bed beneath her made her realize that they'd moved to a bedroom, in a home that she'd not been in before. Her clothing was gone, she wasn't sure when that had happened, but the men were naked as well, their bodies hard—and Christ, were they hard—as they stood over her and fisted their cocks. Neither of them moved; she was sure they were waiting on her to…Lelani wasn't sure what they were wanting her to do. But when she licked her lips, thinking of tasting them, Keion moved closer to the bed and she sat up.

"Just touch me and I'm going to come." Nodding, she reached out and ran her finger along the length of him. "Christ, yes. You're beautiful, and I cannot wait to mark you as ours. I need you, Lelani. So very much."

Her licking the stream of precum from his tip had him moaning. The sound of it was like a finger had touched her from the tip of her toes to her head with warm liquid. Wanting to feel it again, the sensation of his voice, she took him into her mouth just as the bed shifted behind her.

Keion fucked her mouth gently, taking his time and making sure that she wasn't hurt by his cock. She had no idea how she knew this, but as surely as she was sitting there naked, she knew that these men would never hurt her. Never cause her to feel like she was nothing to them. It was a sensation that she'd never experienced before. They cherished her. Wanted her. Needed her.

Their hands were everywhere, her breasts were lifted, her legs spread open. And when fingers slid into her pussy, she cried out and leaned back into Shane, letting go of Keion's magnificent cock as he played with her clit. Keion dropped to his knees in front of her and spread her legs wider. Lelani knew as surely as she was with these two men that they were going to give her such pleasure she might well die from it.

No words were spoken; the men seemed to know just what they were doing, how they were going to take her, give her the most they could. Neither of them rushed her, nor did they try to take more than she was willing to give them. And when Keion, his eyes never leaving hers, leaned to her pussy, he lifted her up by her ass and took her to his mouth. She knew he was going to taste her, to eat her. Cream seemed to flow from her as he blew his warm breath over her heat. When Keion took her to his mouth just as Shane rolled her so that he could take her breasts, Lelani held onto the sheet beneath her and screamed out her release.

The climax was powerful. She screamed a second time when Shane bit down on her breast. Knowing that Keion was drinking from her as fast as she released her cream, her body heated more and she felt her breasts tighten, her nipples painfully so. Shane was suckling at her breast, fondling the other while he did so, tugging at her nipples, and she was so close again that she felt overwhelmed by it.

"Please."

Shane took her mouth and kissed her, his tongue fucking her mouth as Keion was her pussy. She came again and again, her body weak from them. And when she was laid back, her head on the pillow, Shane stood up, his body covered in a fine dew of masculine sweat. She wanted to taste that as well. Reaching for him now, needing to taste him, he backed up.

"As much as I'd love for you to take me into your mouth, you do that and I'm going to come all over you. And the thought of eating you now has me aching with need." The bed shifted under her and Keion kissed her as he joined her on the bed. Shane stood over them, his cock dripping so much that she reached out and touched her fingers to the hot creamy liquid. He moaned then and stepped back before speaking. "My turn."

Chapter 3

Shane wanted to fuck her, slam his cock so deep into her that she'd know that she belonged to them. But the need to taste her, to feel her come in his mouth, was a good way to start without plowing her and no doubt hurting her. Because as needy as he was right now, he knew that he'd hurt her badly. Getting on the bed with her and Keion, he nearly told him to move out of his way, he needed to take her, when she bowed up off the bed in release just from being touched.

It was beautiful. The way her breasts tightened, her nipples, hard as small stones, seemed to pucker more. Her skin took on a pink hue, flushed with her blood, one that had him thinking of pink roses in the summer, wet with the morning dew. And when she begged for more, screamed that she needed it all, he slid his fingers into her pussy and fucked her while Keion ate at her breasts through two more powerful climaxes as he watched her.

He needed her. Now. Shane touched her then, ran his fingers over her breasts to her hips, and over her soft muff of fur. Shane wasn't sure if he could ever think of her again without seeing her just this way. Naked, spread out before him, beautiful.

Keion rolled to his back, his body hard and stiff with need, every line of his body seeming to be in a pleasurable pain right now. As Keion fisted his cock, Shane moved over her. His own cock burned to fill her. Even as he slid his cock over her entrance, feeling her heat, the way she seemed to suck him in, he knew that he'd not last long. When she came, her body hugging his, tightening around him, Shane was going to come with her, empty all that he was deep within his mate.

He told himself to fuck her this way, bring her over with just the crown of his cock inside of her. She would be wetter for him, her body readier. But Shane was dying. He knew this was going to kill him, taking his time with his love.

When she pulled his mouth to hers, he kissed her, tasting her and Keion on her lips. Her hips moved with his crown filling her over and over as he took her. And when she wrapped her legs around his thighs and pushed upward, he slammed forward and felt her climax as it rippled around them.

There was no pausing for her to adjust to his size. He couldn't have stopped now with a gun to his head. She was theirs; Lelani Wayne was their mate and he needed the world to know it. He needed to mark her, to give her what no man had ever been able to before. Love. Love for all the ages.

Shane fucked her hard. He thought of going slower,

making it last, but he saw her face, the need there, and it took him over the edge. Crying out, he bowed back, fucking her deeper, harder than he had before as he emptied himself. And when she screamed out his name, then Keion's, he came a second then a third time as she took him over the edge again with her. When he dropped onto her, hands moved him over, adjusted him on the bed so he was no longer atop her. Keion was moving over her body even as he rolled to his back, and he felt his cock fill again as he watched his other half take their mate. Christ, they were perfect together.

Shane watched her breasts as they moved with each stroke of Keion's cock. The bounce of them, the way that each stroke seemed to make them move quicker. Her fingers danced over his other half's skin as they had his, touching to mark him, to feel that he was real. It was the same thoughts he'd had when he touched her. Shane fisted his cock as he watched them, falling deeply in love with the both of them as the two of them made love. And when she touched her fingers to Keion's mark, Shane felt it as well, like a soft caress over his entire being.

Keion came twice as he fucked their mate, his body bowed back as his had been. Shane leaned over and took her breast into his mouth and bit her hard enough to taste her blood, sucking deeply so that he could bring her once again. Keion came again when she came, his body as hard as the stone of the castle they were working on. Then he simply dropped.

When Keion laid over her, his body moving to make room for him should he want to move to her other side, he lifted up her breast for Keion to feed from. Shane slid his fingers into her pussy when Keion took her breast. They were feasting on her and she didn't seem to mind it at all, he thought with a grin. He loved her…with all his heart, Shane loved her.

He would bring her again then let her rest, he told himself. But when she didn't move again, he lifted his head and realized that she'd fainted. They'd given her all that they had, and it must have been too much. Moving away from her, Shane looked at Keion.

He looked sappy was all he could think of. Shane thought that he sort of felt that way too, like a man who had been given all his most satisfying whims, and every wish he'd ever had was granted. They had a mate. And Christ, she was wonderful.

Looking down at her body, he could see small bruises and cuts that they'd given her. While they'd tried their best to be gentle and careful with her, they'd still injured her. Licking those that he could see closed and kissing the darkening spots made from their fingers, Shane thought of all the things that they'd done to her and how much more he wanted to do. Keion laid back on the bed and smiled at him.

"We really moved fast on this. Do you think she'll be all right?" He looked at the man that he'd spent all his life with and asked him what he meant. "I mean, she knows our names and what we are, but nothing else. I really would like to have had her get to know us a little, wouldn't you? I guess we do have a lifetime to tell her about us, but I think we should have…I don't know, wined and dined her a little."

"You could be right. But I think we needed her too much to make that work. There was the most overpowering need to touch her, mark her as ours. Like if we didn't, we'd lose her or something." Keion told him it was exactly like that, and stood up to dress. "Where are you going?"

"If I stay here, I'm going to take her again and again. I was thinking that...I'm going to go and get her some flowers. Find out if Elbert has some scones or something sweet we can give her when she wakes up. I know it sounds stupid, but—"

"No, no. I think you're right. She needs us to pamper her." He lifted her hand up and showed Keion what he'd discovered when she'd touched him. "She's worked really hard. Hard enough to have calluses, and there are scars here as well. I don't want her to work this hard, not again. What do you suppose she does for a living?"

"I'm going to find out. You're right, I don't want her to think she has to work, not for money. I mean, if it's something she enjoys then she should do it, but we have enough money." Shane agreed with him, but told him they'd never tell her that she had to quit or anything like that. She might get her dander up, as Dad was fond of saying. "We sound like a couple of teenagers with a new toy. I think before we talk to her we should really get our shit together and think things through, don't you?"

Shane agreed. But he knew what Keion meant. It was as if his thoughts were all over the place and not centralized on one thing. He kissed her gently on the forehead, not chancing getting anywhere near her beautiful mouth.

Getting up as well, he dressed and then picked up what was left of her clothing. She was tiny, he realized, and would more than likely be able to wear something from the other women until they could get her something of her own. When he left the bedroom after covering her up and making sure she was all right, he made his way to the kitchen. He was startled to see a man there.

"My name is Roger, her cat. You met me earlier today. I have no last name. I suppose you could call me Roger Lynx, but I've never had an occasion to use it. I think, being a cat as I was, there wasn't anyone to claim me with a surname." Shane nodded, knowing that as her familiar, he would literally belong to her. "She's a witch, you know that, don't you? A very strong one as well."

"I think we figured that out, yes. You're her counterpart." He said he was her familiar. "All right, familiar then. To be honest with you, I'm not sure what that means. The others here, the other witches, they have one as well, but not a shifter like you are."

"I was a cat, just a cat, when she found me. But she needed me to be her man as well. Not sexual, but someone to be stronger for her should she need it. And the other witches, they have someone like me as well. Gobi has a necklace. She touches it when she is nervous. There is magic in it. Ariannona, she has her dragon, the other mate. Caroline, she has one as well. I don't know what it is as I have not met her, but she has one. All witches that are from the time before would have one." Shane thought he meant older witches from his time. "She is your mate then? You and the other one, the dragon, correct? You should know that Lelani, she thinks herself not good enough for a man. That's the doing of her mother and sister. You should know that they were not ever good to her, not like they should have been."

"Why not? And I know they might not have been very

64

forthcoming with their love of her, but why would she think that of herself?" Roger stood up when Shane pulled a glass from the cabinet and took it from him. Shane sat down as Roger went to the refrigerator and pulled out the pitcher of tea, as well as makings for lunch. "You don't have to do that."

"Nay, I do not. But I wish to. It will give me something to do. I have been…she will not use me unless it is unsafe for her. But mostly it is to take care of people who wish her harm, as I said. She doesn't understand why the males of her kind think to touch her, to gaze at her beauty. She doesn't realize how beautiful she is, nor that magic seems to glow around her." Shane asked him if that happened a lot. "Over the years, yes. She is very beautiful, as I have said, but she isn't good around people. Males especially. They don't care for the way she just says what she thinks. I like it, but then I'm more than likely used to it by now. We've been together for a great many years. And crowds, they make her have a panic attack. It's not been much of a problem of late, but today she nearly lost her power. And that would be horrific. She can only be afraid or hold the magic that she's not used much to her. Lelani, as yet, cannot do both. So she gains control or she loses the power."

"Thank you for this. We were just saying how we wished we'd taken things slower. Gotten to know her. I'd like to know everything about her. And soon, we'll have to go into town and pick up things for her. Stuff she might need while here." Roger assured him that she had everything she needed. They had packed well before coming here. "I see. Can you bring her things here? Perhaps yours as well?"

"You wish for me to stay here with you?" Shane told him

that he was his family as well because he was with Lelani. "I will bring her things here; there is very little. I will do as you have asked, but you should speak to her about living here. She doesn't do well around people, as I have said."

"She gets overwhelmed." Roger nodded as he handed him a plate with a thick roast beef sandwich on it, as well as chips. Shane was pretty sure that they'd had neither in the house this morning when he'd left to go to the castle. When he looked at Roger to ask him about it, he sat down across from him with a large steaming hot pizza. "You have magic as well; I'm assuming because of what you are to Lelani."

"Yes. Not as much as my mistress, but enough to feed and clothe us. As I said, we have packed well. We've no need for baggage or foods. Should we need it, Lelani and her magic provides it. Also a home or a place to rest. Money has never been a problem either, though she does have a great deal of it. She does not spend on things that she can't justify." So she didn't need anything because she could conjure it as she needed it. His brother, Elam, could dress himself in much the same manner, but he needed to have the clothing first… they had to be in his drawers or closet before he could wear them. "You will need to know something else about her. She is being pursued by the Herald because of her sister and her ways. They mean to kill her."

"I thought she was dead." He nodded as he ate the last slice of pizza. "Then I'm afraid I don't understand. I know that the Herald is looking for witches to bring to their own kind of justice, but she's protected here by a lot of magic. How is her dead sister involved in this?"

"They were twins, the two of them. No one, save their

mother, could tell them apart that did not know one or the other. While they were exact copies of each other in looks, they were as different as night and day as people. Erin, she craved the limelight. Enjoyed when people knew what she was, what she did. And if they didn't know, she certainly gave them all the details, even ones that she made up to make herself look as if she was more. Her mother was much the same way. And they both took care that Lelani was nowhere near them when they started on their fabrications. They believed that since they were singled out by the king and queen, they were special. I suppose in a small way they were. But we both know that it was her, Lelani, who was special to them." Shane nodded. "You should know that Lelani needs quiet, prefers her own company to being around people, and she doesn't interact well when there is conflict. Her idea to end it is to kill whoever is the meaner of the two. My lady does not tolerate fools well, either. The Herald, they seek her not knowing that she's not Erin. They've not a clue that she's about the most powerful witch there is, either." Shane asked him about Caroline, because he thought she was strong. "Yes. I've known her. And she is strong as well. But my Lelani? She would mop the floor with her should it come to that."

Shane was still sitting there, just thinking, after Roger left to get their truck. It had been parked, he told him, not far from their land. When he looked around after a bit, he noticed Keion sitting across from him with dozens of roses and several tins that he was sure were filled with treats, and that made him laugh. Getting down something to put the flowers in, he told Keion what he'd found out from Roger.

"So, as we thought, they'll come here to try and find them. Do you suppose they know where she is? I mean, I doubt very much if she's this strong, that they'd be able to keep tabs on her unless she let them. She'd know to make herself safe." Shane agreed. "I was by the castle not long ago. Asher said that he could use our help if we'd like to come by. I told him that I'd see what you wanted to do."

They both turned to the doorway when they heard someone there. Lelani was dressed in a long skirt and vest and very little else. He wondered briefly if she had on panties when she moved toward them with a limp. Pulling out a chair for her, he took her foot in his hand when she said she'd hurt it.

"I took a little tumble in the bathroom. It's not.... I hope you don't mind, but I made it just a little bigger than it was. I can put it back should you not care for it." Shane looked over at Keion and he grinned. "Or not. I don't really care. I don't think I'll be here that much longer anyway, do you?"

"Why not?" She said that people were looking for her. "Yes. The Herald. They're looking for all witches. I don't know what sparked them to life again, but they've been out and about making trouble for a few. I think, total, there are about nine of them living on this land. Witches, I mean. Also, I wanted to tell you about the others. The other dragons besides the family."

"Roger told me." She pulled her foot out of his hands and stood up. "And about the other witches. I know that they're here. I can feel them. A couple of them, you should know, don't belong here. They're witches, but have been promised things that won't be delivered to them if they tell these people

68

what they know about this place and the people here. The witches think to profit off the death of their sisters by keeping tabs on what is going on, the ways in and out of here, as well as how many people are not human. They're especially supposed to find out all they can about Erin, who I don't think they know has already been killed. Or if they've heard, they don't believe it. They've seen me."

"You mean that these witches are working for the Herald?" She said that they were working with someone. "Can you tell me which ones? We can't have trouble here. We have enough of that as it is with dragon slayers and anyone else that thinks to come here for personal gain."

"I don't know them by name, only that they're here with the idea that killing a witch will give them their powers." He asked her if it would. "To a point. But you cannot kill us without reason. I mean, simply because you want their powers, perhaps, but you can't kill for a profit. That's what it would be should they take the money from the men that seek us and then kill."

"You mean they must follow the rules too, even in this?" She nodded and put a cup on the table. With a touch of her fingers, the cup was filled with hot tea. Lelani asked them if they'd like a cup before they left. "We're leaving?"

"Yes. The castle needs to be finished. Now. I need to go and make that happen before it's too late."

~~~

Keion wasn't sure what he was supposed to do. Lelani told him to stand behind her but not to touch her yet. It was the most difficult thing he'd been asked to do. But then, she'd

69

not asked. He was beginning to think it was the way she did things all the time, just tell you what needed done and expect you to comply. It wasn't that she was rude, but she knew how it was to work and didn't care for anyone messing with her ideas.

"I'm sorry. But once more. We're going to do this how?" Asher looked at him and Shane when Lelani told him it was time to get the south wall up. "And why this wall only? I was under the impression that we had to build the walls up a layer at a time."

Daniel moved to stand beside them now, as had several of the other larger dragons. They seemed to understand the progression of things better than they did, but Keion didn't ask again. He thought himself stupid for not understanding what she wanted.

"Okay, first of all...." She turned to him. "You're not stupid. And if you say that again, I'm going to hurt you. You're ignorant of this process. That does not make you stupid. You just don't know. Got it?"

"Yes." He kissed her then and she told him to behave. "Trust me when I tell you, I am. What I really want to do is take you over to that flat stone, lay you out naked, and take you. This is me appeasing myself with a kiss and not fucking you hard out here in the open where anyone can see us."

He might have been pleased with the look on her face if he wasn't afraid of her. Not that she'd hurt him, but she was having some trouble controlling her magic. He wasn't sure why and neither were the rest of them, but he'd bet it was because she had so much and rarely used it. The fact that she had no control over it was something that he was going to ask her about too. Why didn't she use what had been given to her? Asher cleared his throat.

"Okay, the south wall. I don't know. I mean, all I know is that it has to be up before nightfall. And as your mates aren't here to help me with that, the dragons will." Asher looked at the line of dragons, then back at her. "I'm going to use them. Not completely, I'd never do that, but they're going to enrich my magic for me. But I need for you to stay out of the way or risk being harmed. And by harmed I mean crushed under the weight of a stone that could easily weigh about seventy tons."

It was then that Keion got it. They weren't going to help lift, they were going to let her use a part of their magic to get the wall up. And only the older dragons, like Daniel and a few others. They were able to help because it would be very draining on the younger ones who had less magic, and since the older ones had the most power, she would use them enough to make this work.

But it wasn't just the help of magic that she was going to need. He and Shane were there to give her whatever she desired. Mostly she told him to catch her when she fell, and she would. And also to make sure that she wasn't down too long without replenishments. That was where her familiar came in.

Elbert brought the coolers from the truck. Caroline and Gobi exited the other side. He wasn't sure what was going to happen between the witches. He'd noticed that they were a very solitary type, so he moved closer to Lelani when Shane did as the other two approached her. They seemed to be sizing each other up, trying to see who was the baddest there. Then

71

when both Caroline and Gobi bowed, Keion was pretty sure that they'd just acknowledged that Lelani was.

"We've come to help." Lelani shook her head. "Okay, let me say this another way. We would like to lend you our power. I've also instructed Elbert and Jacob to stand by with juice and fruit, and there is fresh meat for the dragons when you're done. You'll need us for no other reason than we're going to be drained anyway, so we might as well be here."

"I won't take from the others. It's not right, and I have no wish to hurt you." Caroline nodded and thanked her for that. "They'll feel it, the women who just gave birth, but they won't be harmed by it. I only know that this needs to be done."

"Elbert left them juices as well, both of them. Lindsey is upset that she cannot be here, but she knows that the babe needs her more. And Essie is setting up a place for the others to come when they're ready. Her little girl is doing well, thanks to you." Keion felt Lelani's embarrassment, but didn't say anything. She'd given something to Essie when she'd been in labor, he thought. To keep her healthy. "If you're ready, we're ready."

Ariannona joined them then, with hundreds of faeries and brownies. They bound together, forming great circles around Lelani but never touching her. Whatever they were lending her, apparently it had to be done as a group. Lelani told everyone there that she was as ready as she'd ever be.

When she lifted her arms up he thought of last night, when he'd had the vision of tying her up so that they could both have their way with her. But when the trees swayed a little at first, then a little more, he saw the way the dragons moved closer to her. He touched her arms when he was told to, as did Shane. The pulse of energy was powerful, and draining as well. He could only imagine what she was taking from the dragons when he felt slightly nauseous and weak at just a small touch.

The energy burning off her was hot. Almost too much, he thought, for a woman without a dragon. He ran hot, being what he was, and would be hotter still when he was in his other form. But to see her like this, feel her heat, he wondered at how much magic she did indeed have.

It was then that the rocks that had been brought from the quarry started to move, their weight nothing to the magic that lifted them and moved them quietly into position as if they were held by a magical string. As they watched, keeping a safe distance back, the wall that they'd been working on began to take shape. The earth below it moved, making room for the stone, to make sure that it was tight against the stone wall behind it.

They'd raised the walls several stones high over the last several weeks, and recently had started seeing the shape of the castle taking its ending form. Having cleared out all the lower levels inside the fallen castle, and with the stone that they were going to use in neat piles, they knew it was going to be a long hard haul to finish. They'd been lifting the stones, with the help of all the larger dragons, and putting them in place to form the foundation of what would be the main part of the castle, but it was slow, difficult work.

As he watched Lelani work to bring the stones to the base, he could see windows form in the stone that hadn't been accounted for just yet. There was a fireplace, he realized, on the wall in the drawings, and it was formed too. Shelves that had been carved from the stone in the other castle were there as well. Improvements too, some of them small but noticeable, and larger ones, like the longer hearth and the stone indentations to hold extra wood. It was almost as if she'd been here or had looked in the books they'd found.

Daniel dropped to the ground. She'd told him that she'd use him first so that he could rest the longest in the event she needed him again, and it looked to have been a little too much for him. He was an old dragon, brother to Keion's mom, actually. But in that moment, Keion knew that she'd not used him up, not entirely, and wouldn't go back to use him again if she could help it. She'd given him his dignity in this, his self-worth, by using him as her first bit of power to show all that watched that he was still a dragon worth having around. Keion fell in love with her all over in that moment.

For all her professed hatred of people, she'd done this for him. Of course, Daniel wasn't a person, but a dragon, but he was still their friend. He watched as two more of the dragons fell to the earth, their bodies heaving with exhaustion while the castle moved and became complete...as complete as it could be right now.

Others still began to drop in exhaustion. Caroline and Gobi were waning but never moved away, but did take juice and fruit when it was handed to them. Even as his brothers began to falter, Lelani never stopped, didn't lower her hands or stop the movement of the stones. The need to have this wall complete no matter what clawed at her, and in turn him and Shane as well.

After several more minutes, the wall was up. Not only

that, but he could see where the other stones would fit, the way the opening for the door had been carved by magic, and there were shutters for the windows she'd put in, for winter months as well as wind. Her magic had done more in one hour than they'd done over the last month. Christ, it was going to be beautiful here when they were done.

When she staggered a little, he and Shane caught her. Asher had fallen to the earth, his body covered in a fine sweat, as had the others, but they were otherwise fine. The only ones that remained standing other than the three of them were Caroline and Akassa, his brother. Picking Lelani up in his arms, Shane took her to the ground as well and Keion joined them, looking at the wall.

He knew that the castle was going to be large. But to see this single wall, the turret on it there as well, he was blown away by the sheer size of it. The stone looked as if it had been carved from a single rock, no small cracks in it to mar its beauty, nor did the window openings looked crooked or misaligned. Standing up, he moved to stand next to it and put his hand upon it. He felt the heat under his hand and asked about it. As Lelani explained, he went back to sit with her. Everything, even breathing, was exhausting to him, he realized then.

"The earth has decided that there should be no reason for you to ever be cold. And in the summer months, it will be cooler in the castle for those that live there. The windows that are on this side, they're high enough up so that they can't be used as an entry point as well." When Lelani yawned again, he did as well. "Someone is coming." And with that, she fell asleep.

"Someone is coming? That's all we get?" Asher looked upset, but he didn't get up just then. If Keion was honest, he wasn't sure he could do it again, and wondered if the person coming was going to harm them. "You do know that we're all dead should someone really be coming. And if they have a knife or sword, I don't think I could even fend them off with my hands, much less my body."

"She didn't mean now. She meant soon." Caroline stood up and brushed her dress off. Then she turned to him and Shane. "Do you have any idea of the kind of power it took to do this? I don't mean just the moving of the stone—you could have done that—but this is a fortress now. There is no way, even with all our magic, that we could have done even half of what she's done here today. This looks just as it did when your parents were here. The magic used here, it's not just old but ancient. Whatever they gave her, it was enriched by whatever magic she had as well. She is, I believe, the queen of witches everywhere."

The queen? Keion could see that. But right now he was looking at the wall that they'd all had a hand in putting up. As he'd noticed earlier, the walls were perfectly straight, the windows in line and square. The turret, which he knew was copied on each of the four corners, was just as he'd seen in the drawings. A place to put men should the need arise. He could not wait to see it all complete, to stand there now, high above the grounds, and see it just as his parents had long ago.

Caroline drained four glasses of juice before she moved to the wall. When Asher joined her, they walked around the entire thing twice before coming back to sit with them. Asher looked pleased, even excited. It was then that Keion realized what she'd meant by it being a fortress. The walls were thicker than he'd realized, and he'd bet higher too. She had anticipated that they'd have to go to war sometime. Looking at her sleeping in Shane's arms, he wondered what else she could do. Hell, what else they could do. He looked around the group.

"Whatever is coming, we needed this to protect us. Or the castle." Caroline said that's what she'd guess too. "How does she know this? I mean, did the earth tell her? Does she know something that we don't?"

"I would say that is all about right. Yes, the earth will speak to her. Not on the same level as it will Essie and Asher or the rest of you, but she can talk to it. Does she know something you don't? I would say that she knows a great deal more than any of us do. You mustn't forget that she was touched by the king and queen. They were able to foretell things as well, know that they had to ready you for their death. Did she get a part of that? I would say so." Caroline looked at Lelani. "She's stronger than even I was told she'd be. Stronger even than she knows. I believe that she would be considered the most powerful witch ever born. And in that, she's going to be sought after as if she were carrying her weight in gold. The Herald, they'll come for her now. Fixing this building, someone will feel this and tell them about it."

"She said that there were witches here that were trying to make a profit off all of you being here. Is it one of them?" Caroline closed her eyes before answering him. He was almost afraid of her answer. So when she looked at him and nodded, he wanted to go out and find them and make them leave here now.

"Will do you no good, I'm afraid. The damage is done. The Herald won't be able to enter the land, thankfully, but their troops are here now. They'll try to harm us in ways that only magic can." He asked her what they could do now. "I don't know…I honestly don't know, Keion. But she will, and it will not be a gentle fight. I have no idea why I think that, but it's as true as me standing here. It will be a bloody and horrific fight. But it will also be quick, harsh, and violent for those witches."

Both Shane and Keion carried her back to their home. Lelani didn't weigh much, but they both wanted to hold her, so they switched back and forth for the opportunity to do so. When they entered the house, Roger was waiting for them. Once they had her in the bedroom that they all would share, he brought them both a lunch of thick sandwiches and a cooler full of a variety of juices.

"Lelani prefers fresh, so if you don't mind, I'm going to have one of the others plant a few trees in the yard for her. I'll tend to them." Shane told him to go ahead. "Also, there is the matter of me sleeping here. I would request the room on the lower level, below the ground. There is a nice door there for me, and my own yard, if you please. I can come and go as I need to. I should also like to have a garden of my own. Not that I don't like what the others grow, but I have my own tastes, as does my mistress."

After he was given permission to do whatever he needed, Shane turned to Keion after Roger left them. "There wasn't a lower level. We didn't have a basement either, much less an entrance for him to go into his own backyard." Keion laughed. Things were certainly moving along, he thought.

Chapter 4

Robert tried to think. There were just too many people talking at once for him to get a single thought straight in his head. They had found her, that much he'd gotten. But the part he was having a hard time wrapping his head around was that she'd moved a mountain. Pulling out his gun, he fired two shots into the air before they all settled down again. It ruined the plaster, of course, but right now he wanted their full attention. He was pretty sure he had it.

The witch that stood before him only laughed, Robert decided that he disliked her most of all of the witches that he'd killed over the last six months. She had a knowing look on her face, and he found that he wanted to slap it off her every time he saw her. But he'd not let her rattle him, not again. He needed her much more than she needed him, and he never wanted her to figure that out. But he was pretty sure it was too late for that.

"What do you mean, she moved a mountain? Surely you jest." She shook her head. "Then explain yourself. I don't have time for this foolishness. How the hell do you expect me to believe that she moved a fucking mountain, when I can't get the neighbor's dog to stop shitting in my yard every day?"

"Perhaps you should kill it as you do most things in your life that you dislike. The castle, the one I told you about, she went out there with the others and finished an entire wall of it by moving the stones into place with her magic. Of course we all felt it...she drained us a little when she took from us. Wasn't stealing however, which would have gotten her into a great deal of trouble with the higher ups, if there were any. As part of our deal of living there, we were to give when needed. I had to give to her." He asked her how this was even possible. "Magic. I told you that she was strong, but you'd not believe me when I told you how strong. She is going to be your downfall too, I think. And mine."

"You'll tell her who we are?" The woman, her name was Cybil he thought, told him that she more than likely knew them by now, not just by name but everything she wanted to know about them. "I don't think so. We keep a very low profile, and in that, no one knows who we are."

"You're sure about that?" He nodded, but her question made him think. "The Heralds have been around for longer than most buildings in this town. And what they don't know about them directly has been made up in stories and tales to keep other witches in line. It's one of the first things they tell us about when we come into our own. Don't be caught by the Herald. But you'd know that, wouldn't you? You're a descendant of them, aren't you?"

Robert leaned back in his seat and regarded the witch in front of him. She knew a great deal for a mere witch. He was ready to have her taken away when she laughed at him. The sound of it, so scary-like, actually made him reach down to cup his balls.

"Rohm was my too many great-grandfather to count back. He and his wife, they had several daughters and one son. But the son was murdered by a witch one night when they were supposed to be burning her at the stake. I'm not sure about that part, but that's the story." Cybil shook her head and said that no witch killed him. "Yes, she did. Mary Wayne was responsible for his death, as well as Rohm's. Everyone knows that story."

"Lies. They were fed to you and others by Rohm to gather enough men to go after her. To make themselves appear to be stronger than they were. But it never worked; he could never get to her after that night. It was said that a man only had to cross the barrier to the land that she'd been given to protect her to have his male parts shrivel up and die." He'd heard that as well. He no more believed that than he did a woman was actually burned at the stake because she was a witch. "But Rohm's new wife killed him, just as the son's own wife murdered him. They had found out about the others, you see. The women that he'd fuck on his altar and then claim that they'd tricked him. Children, too, were born to them; I'm thinking you might be descended from one of them. Trick her once, shame on them, trick her several hundred times.... Well, I think you understand. He was responsible for Mary's

83

death indirectly, but unless he did it from the grave, he never lived to see it. His wife, fat with another daughter, gave birth the day after he died, just as Mary's curse said he would. He would never see another of his children born."

"My ancestor was a godly man." Again the laughter. "He did kill Mary. The story goes that he caught her with a man between her legs and killed him. Then he took her to the church grounds and put her there himself and burned her. As should have happened when he captured her after her making claims about his son. She claimed that he raped her, and Michael said that she'd used her powers over him to make her carry his child."

"There was a babe, yes. And it *was* fathered by Rohm's son, as Mary claimed. But Mary and her babe were safe on the land given to her by the king and queen of dragons. It is said, and this part I know not if it is true, that the queen had need of her child. She had none of her own and she paid Mary to birth her one. But soon after that, the castle fell and the king and queen were murdered. So Mary's children—there were two of them—had been blessed with magic by the queen so they were safe, so long as they followed the rules on the grounds given to her that night." Robert told her that she lied, that there was no way she could know this. "But I do. As does every witch that has ever come after Mary. She lives even now, the daughter of Michael Herald and Mary Wayne. One was recently murdered, as you well know, but the—"

"You speak of dragons and kings and queens like they are real. You said that she lives now, this child of his. You know as well as I do that isn't possible. She would be centuries old, shriveled up and deep in her grave. There isn't any way for her to be there unless she's a ghost too." She said that she lived and was as beautiful as anyone she'd ever met. "I don't know why I'm even listening to you. You're stupid if you believe even half of what you're saying.

"Believe what you wish, but I know what I've seen. It was a full thirteen years after his son's death before Mary was murdered, and your sire did not do the murdering. She was killed by her own child, her firstborn, by telling the Herald where she was." Robert was more confused now than when he'd tried to read over his long dead grandfather's notes. There had been no mention of a child. None either of a dragon king and queen. This woman had no idea what she was talking about. "When you go there, Robert, make sure that you have your affairs in order, your will made out. And that any child that you have is safe as well. The curses that she will put upon you will make you wish you had followed in your sire's footsteps and died an early death."

After he had her taken away, laughing and telling him to get his affairs in order, Robert pulled out his family's notes. He'd found them several years ago in his grandmother's attic, and had been reading and rereading them since. She'd told him that for a long while his dad had written in the journal, but she'd long since put it away. No one had touched it in many years, but some of the dates on it were thousands of years ago. But it was his grandmother's words that he remembered now.

"Nothing but stupidity if you ask me. Why do any of us care that someone can mix a few herbs together and come up with a cure for some foot fungus? Or that they think themselves magical at all? There is no such thing as magic, Robert. Remember that if you remember nothing else that I have said to you. It just does not exist; it cannot." He had asked her for the book and she said she didn't care. But he'd been forbidden to take it from her home. Her thinking was that he could sell it someday, the ramblings of a fool, for enough money to go to college. "You mark my words. Someday someone is going to pay you a lot of money for that thing. You keep it nice while you're here and we'll laugh all the way to the bank about it; see if we don't, my boy. Magic. Next thing you know, they'll be telling us that you can pull a real rabbit from your ass. Stupid people."

Robert had thought her wrong but had never told her that. She was old, set in her ways. She hadn't even owned a cordless phone, preferring instead to have one attached to the wall with a long cord that got wrapped up in things when you used it. When he went to visit her she'd make him do the oddest things, too. Salt had to be around each window and door, with no break in the lines. He was never to wear his shoes in the house. He was never allowed to eat after midnight either. All these rules. And when he asked her why or why not, she told him that was the way she liked it. It wasn't until later, when he'd been a grown man, that he realized that his grandmother did believe in magic. Or at least she'd been afraid of it. And each of her rules were to keep any kind of magic from entering her home. She had been keeping herself safe, but he never figured out from what or who.

Opening the book to where the first entries were, he read the words there. Or he tried to. His ancestor, Rohm, could neither spell well nor finish a sentence that made any sense.

Most of the time he'd read his entries over and over and have a headache afterwards that would make him sick to his belly. The man had been an idiot.

"Mary Wain cae to hose toda. Sad my boe had taked what she had and filed her belie with a babe."

He worked at figuring it out and came up with Mary went to Rohm's house and claimed that Michael Herald, his son, had raped her and now she was having his baby. As he went on, translating it to what he thought it said, he came to the part about the man and woman who had been mentioned by Cybil. There was no mention of them being anything but that, a man with his wife. He had mentioned that he'd felt peculiar, but not why or how it had happened. Then he told about the curse and his son being murdered.

Robert supposed that Michael Herald's wife might have killed him. He certainly would have been tempted had he known the man, he thought. There were many mentions throughout the book about how others had come forth, trying to claim a bit of the family fortune by saying that they were a child of his. Not that there was much in the way of fortune. Even one of the sisters had said that, saying that he'd ruined them for any husband. Hell, he was one of the bastards, just as the witch had guessed about him.

Yet there was no mention of his daughters, no names associated with the family in the big book that he could find either. It was as if they were never important enough for the writer to even bother with remembering anything about them. Robert had had to unearth a family Bible that had been written in over the centuries before he was even able to trace his own line back far enough to see which daughter had started his family tree. He was indeed a descendant of Rohm Herald, but from Rachel, the second daughter, who had never married as far as he could see. If the younger daughters had had sons, there was no mention of them either. It was as if the entire line had died other than the bastards of either man.

He looked at the clipping of Michael Herald's death. The person who had written this piece of drivel had had no better spelling ability than Rohm, and whatever they didn't have in that department, they made up for in prose. According to the obituary, Michael Herald, was a sainted man who had angels on his shoulders and might have had some sort of direct connection with the good Lord himself. Robert wondered if the man's father had dictated it for the person that had put it in the local paper, and thought perhaps, if the townspeople had been asked, there would be an entirely different accounting of the man. No man, no matter how good they appeared, was as good as Michael's obit had claimed.

He was still reading through the book when his son came to get him for dinner. Picking the boy up in his arms, he and Mark headed for the dining room. The doorbell was ringing as he went by it, and he answered it with a smile on his face. The woman standing there threw him off.

"May I help you?" She moved by him and into the room where he was. Not by him so much as through him. He rubbed his body where he imagined her touching him, and decided that he'd been reading too much and was going to limit himself from now on. Putting his son down, he ordered him to go to his mother and to call the police. Then he turned to the woman standing by his staircase. "You weren't invited in. I'd very much like it if you were to leave now."

"No, I wasn't, was I? But I'm not really here, anyway. You can see me because I wish it so. However, if the police come and you point me out to them, they're more than likely going to take you away to a padded cell. Do they do that still?" She sat down on air and he felt his heart start to pound. "Have a seat, Robert. What I have to say is going to knock you on your ass a few times, and I'd rather not have to worry that you'll not be listening. Oh, and your son and wife, they think that you've forgotten something in your office and will join them momentarily. And the police have not been called in. So, it's just you and I until I say what I have to tell you."

The chair bumped him in the back of his legs, and he'd had no choice but to fall into it. When he started to rise up, he realized that he couldn't. And when his wife came into the front hall with him, she walked right by him saying his name, as if she'd not seen him sitting there.

"As I said, we have to talk. My name is Lelani. I'm a witch. Just in case you might have misheard me, yes, I'm a witch." When she snapped her fingers, he looked down his body to see that he was naked. Then before he could ask her what the hell was going on, he was dressed again. "That was just to show you that I don't need to be in the room with you to make you see all sorts of things. By the way, I can make you do shit too, so don't fuck with me. I'm not in the best of humor. Not that I am normally, but today isn't going to bode well for you should you rile me up more."

"What do you want? Money? Well, you're shit out of luck. I'm not giving you anything." She said she knew that, he

89

didn't have any. "Then what is it you want? You think to come here and warn me off one of your friends? Well, I'm carrying on my family work in ridding the world of your kind."

"My kind? I think I might have heard that some other time in my life. Cybil, she might have mentioned to you that I'm old, and I think she might have told me that you think of us as beneath you. But, I'll be three thousand years old in a couple of years. I'm telling you that because I know that men in this era aren't supposed to ask how old a woman is. Stupid, but there it is." He started to ask her what sort of drugs she was on when she laughed. "I'm not on drugs, you moron. First because they have no effect on me, and secondly, I've no need for them to make me tell you the truth. And so you are aware, Cybil won't be helping you anymore. Helping anyone for that matter."

"You killed her? Not possible. She was a strong witch. But you might have saved me the trouble. Cybil said that you moved a mountain today." She shrugged at his statement. "How the hell can you expect me to believe that? No one moves mountains."

"I suppose, should I really want to, I could with the help of the earth. Should she not be too busy at other things. But really, I only moved stones. Large ones, yes, but stones all the same. The castle needed to be reinforced. I was lucky enough to have the dragons there with me, or I might not have been able to finish it." He said that Cybil had not mentioned any dragons. "No, she wouldn't have. I didn't want her to see them, so she didn't. I'm telling you that they were there to prove a point."

"What point would that be? That you can make stones

move with the help of dragons? There is no such thing as dragons, nor is there any way for you to have moved stones. With or without their help. You might very well be a witch, but they cannot move things like you're talking about, and they most certainly cannot believe in dragons. They use trickery and slight of hand, taking advantage of men and women for money. That is the reason that I'm working to rid the world of them." She tsked at him. "If you are indeed a witch, you're going to be caught soon. And while we don't burn your kind at the stake anymore, I can tell you that you'll suffer just as much. There are several ways to kill a witch, as I'm sure you know."

"Yes, there are. And so many ways for you to die as well." She stood up and leaned over him. He watched as her face changed, morphed into first his wife then his son before she stood up again as Lelani. "You killed her too, didn't you, Robert James? I know that you're not really a Herald. You changed your name when you were seventeen because you found out that you might be related to a monster. And using that name and his works, you felt justified in killing young Beth when you found this wife more to your needs. Of course you did try her out, didn't you? Had an affair with her nearly the entire time you were married to poor Beth. She was no more a witch than you are a human being. You, too, are nothing but a monster. Stop killing things you have no understanding of, Robert. Should you continue—well, I should say when you continue, because we both know that you're not going to stop—but I will kill you. Not maybe, I will. Don't make me have to come back here."

When he looked around after she left him, Robert saw that he was in the dining room of his home. His wife of eight years was staring at him as if she'd never seen him before, and his son was looking at him with his spoon poised at his mouth, as if he'd been interrupted in taking a bite. When he asked them what was going on, his wife put down her cup and cleared her throat.

"You were talking. About dragons and mountains. I don't think that is appropriate dinner conversation, do you?" He shook his head and asked her where she'd gone. "She who? There was never anyone here, Robert. You just came in, sat down, and started talking about this other person. About witches and burning them at the stake. Who is she? What does she have to do with what you were saying before? Or is it that you're trying to upset me? Have you been reading that book again? Is that what this is all about? Please just throw the thing out, will you? I don't like that nasty thing being in this house. I think it might have germs."

He looked around again. They were alone in his dining room, and apparently he'd been here for a bit. The glass of water that was served at every meal, even though he wanted tea, was half empty, his plate devoid of the meat on it yet still holding all the vegetables; Brussels sprouts again, with carrots that were untouched. He'd lifted his napkin to see if he'd put his meatloaf there when he realized what Lynne had said to him about the book.

"I can't throw that out. It's been in my family for generations. It has our history in it." She picked up her glass of water then and sipped it with a pinched look on her face. "Lynne, you have to understand, I need to carry on the

92

work of my ancestors. They were on a mission, and I need to complete it."

"I don't want to talk about it anymore. If you must have it around, take it out to the garage. Or better yet, to your office. I don't want it here, Robert." As she bent over her salad, he looked at his son. He loved the boy to pieces, but he was pretty sure he thought he was nuts too. His own family was turning against him. Robert wondered if this was what it had been like for Rohm. "Did you hear me, Robert? Take it out of my house."

"Yes, dear." He looked around when the laughter echoed in the room. His wife continued to eat, his son played with his food. He started to ask if they'd heard it as well and decided that he might be better off not to. And he wasn't taking the book out of his house, damn it.

~~~

Shane rolled to his back to see that he was alone in the big bed. This was the second morning in a row that he'd found himself like this, and he wasn't happy about it. He wanted to make love to Lelani before starting his day, not have to find her and take her then. Smiling, he got up and went to the bathroom, only to find it being used.

Lelani was on her knees in front of Keion, the water running over them forgotten. Keion's cock was in her mouth and she was holding his balls in her hands as she bobbed up and down over him. Shane felt his own cock stretch at the sight, and leaned against the counter to watch them. Christ, watching her suck off Keion was almost as good as having her go down on him. As he fisted his own cock, he thought about all the ways he was going to take her when it was his turn, and felt his balls tighten to his body. Holy shit, without even touching her, he was ready to explode.

When she stood up suddenly he thought he'd interrupted them. The look on her face, the ruby redness of her lips, made his body burn to be with her. And when she told him to join them, he wasn't sure how that was going to work, but he was all for it. So he entered the shower stall with them.

The water was turned off and he pressed her back against the wall. Then he leaned down and took her breast into his mouth, as Keion did. She held them both to her by fisting their cocks. He watched her hands as he suckled from her and rocked harder into her warm wet palm. He was so close to coming this way that he nearly did when she moaned.

"I want you both. Now. I'm so needy that I could come right now like this." He slid his fingers down to her pussy and pinched her clit. When she cried out, he felt her fingers tighten on his cock, and he nearly came when she did. "Please, I need both of you. I hurt with my need, and you're not helping me."

"Oh, I'm going to help you, Lelani. I'm hoping to help us all." Keion moved out of the shower stall and sat on the counter with one of the towels under his ass while Shane brought her a second time. "We're both going to have fun with you."

"Come here, baby. Come and finish what you started. Then Shane can fuck you." Shane moaned when she moved toward Keion. Her hips swayed, her breasts bounced. Watching her in the mirror in front his other half, all Shane could think about was fucking her, his cock pounding her hard over and over.

When she leaned over Keion, taking him in her mouth again, Shane moved up behind her. He wanted to eat her, taste the juices that he knew were there, but the thought of fucking her while she sucked off Keion made his cock stretch and thicken more. As soon as she spread her legs, he slid his cock into her gently. She was as wet as the walls in the stall, and hotter than any water coming from the faucets.

He fucked her slowly, taking his time as he watched her mouth move over Keion. His body was bowed back on the counter, his hands holding her head over him. Shane could see her breasts move with each of his strokes, the way her nipples were hard as stone. And when he reached to take one of them into his hand, she cupped her own hand around his and squeezed his hand under hers.

Shane held her to him with his free hand as he took her harder. She was moaning now, begging Keion to give her his cum. And when he came, Lelani lifted her head up as cum sprayed her face, and it took Shane over the edge with her. Shane felt like she'd unleashed a madman within him, and he pulled her up from Keion and fucked her pressed against the wall when he turned them into it.

Coming in her this way was strange; wonderful, but strange all the same. She screamed out that she was coming again and Shane joined her, his body feeling like it was being turned inside out with hers. The connection between them, the three of them, gave him an almost inside look into how they were all feeling when she came a second, then a third time in as many minutes. Shane bit down on her shoulder, feeling his mouth fill not just with her blood but her flesh as well. The magic, he could taste it on her, and felt his cock empty once again.

As his body began to slow, his heartrate going back to normal, he looked over at Keion as he laid his head back on the mirror with his eyes closed. He looked every bit as spent as Shane felt. Every cell in his body was drained. He was sure that should they be attacked right now, neither of them could even lift their arms to defend themselves. Christ, she was going to kill them both at this rate. And what a fucking fantastic way to go.

Letting her go was the hardest thing he'd done in his life, but he had to shower and get going. Asher and the others were already at the castle, he was sure. They were hoping to get a lot more of the castle finished before winter set in, which was only three months away.

The three of them ended up in the stall again, but instead of making love, they helped each other clean up. He discovered that bathing with her and Keion wasn't as weird as he'd thought it would be. When Shane stepped out first, he was drying off when he heard Roger calling to them from the lower level. As he dressed and made his way down, Keion joined him.

"There has been a disturbance, my lords." Shane asked him what sort of disturbance. "Your brother, Jed, came by to ask that you join him on the castle grounds. He said that it is important. I'm sorry, that's all he said, but he did seem slightly shocked by whatever was happening."

The two of them were making their way over there when Keion asked him what was going on, and why hadn't they just reached out to them. Shane didn't know but would find out. However, the closer they got to the castle, the slower their steps became. Someone or something had been very busy throughout the night. And when they joined the others who were standing in front of it, he could see by the looks on their faces that they had no idea how it had happened either.

The walls were up. Not finished yet, but nearly so. The stone was splintered in places, didn't quite fit in others, but it looked like they'd only have to put a few more of the massive rocks up to get the entire building done. When he reached out to put his hand on the new stone, Asher stopped him.

"It'll drain you. I mean, you will be down before you can take your hand away." He asked him what he meant, and Asher pointed to Gideon and Simeon as they lay on the grass. "I found them like this, sleeping it off. And when I woke Onimia, who is over there by the way, he said all they'd done was touch the wall and it zapped them like they'd been standing in water and touched a socket."

"What the hell is doing this?" None of them had any idea, but they did keep their distance from the place. As they watched, two more pieces as big as them slid into place. Shane took another step back as he continued. "This is about as strange as it gets. Do you think...Christ, this is gonna sound weird, but do you think that it's doing it all on its own?"

"It's the earth. Now that the wall is up, it feels the need to finish it." Shane pulled Lelani into his arms after Keion kissed her. "If you touch it, if we all touch it a little at a time, it'll finish faster. As it is now, it's borrowing from everyone just a little at a time until it has the energy to move. I'm not saying we should do it; I'm just telling you what it would need to do the work all by itself."

"Is this why you needed to get the wall up?" Asher wasn't looking at her when she shook her head and asked again. "If it is, then it would have been nice to know. Maybe we could have delayed this until we got this over with about the Herald coming around."

"You think I'd drain a few hundred people and creatures to help you put up a castle faster? You're a moron. I didn't do this for the castle to be finished. It's because of this." As they walked around the south side of the castle, he could see what had happened. Had the wall not been there, then everything that they'd done would have been lost. More than likely even going backwards in the process.

The tree that had tumbled down from near the top of the tall mountain lay under several tons of earth and stone. It looked as if the tree had rolled down the hill and picked up loose items as it went. As it grew bigger and bigger, it picked up more debris until it hit the wall. Having the wall there, as massive and complete as it was, kept any debris from falling into the ground work that they'd only just begun. Shane would bet anything that if they'd been working when it fell, someone would have been hurt badly too.

"And the walls going up today...do you know what that is?" Lelani said she didn't know, but it was nice, wasn't it? "Yes. It's wonderful, but I'd like to know who I have to thank for this. It's saved us a great deal of work."

"I would say your wives, yours and Jed's." Shane asked her if they'd done it. "No, but the babes are going to be safer within these walls than out if trouble comes. The earth, it knows that a princess has been born, and a new dragon speaker as well. The wall that we all built, it was to save the castle; they're saving the children. Sometimes the earth does things because it knows better than a person does. You should think of that sometimes before you speak. Or not speak at all. That would make me happy."

Shane laughed, but covered it with a cough when Asher pinned him with a look. It was funny to him the way that he and Lelani went at each other all the time. Shane had asked her if she hated his brother, and she'd assured him it was just too much fun not to get him going. He supposed that everyone had to have some fun.

"Is something coming? You said that, that someone was coming." Lelani nodded, but didn't answer when Essie and the other women joined them. Shane wanted answers, but he wasn't sure what the questions would be just now. He was so excited about the castle being complete that his mind couldn't wrap around the person coming.

"I think we have to sit down and talk, all of us. There are things going on, underhanded things, that you need to be made aware of. While the dragons here are safe, I've taken precautions in keeping the others unaware. But it's time I told you about my sister and mother." Asher nodded, but said nothing as he held his wife. Essie looked beautiful, and Lindsey nearly glowed with good health. He wondered if it was the earth doing that, or if Lelani had a lot to do with it.

As they made their way to the big house, Shane wondered about the things she was going to tell them. He knew about the Heralds and their clan. He also knew a little about her family history. Not much, but enough that he knew that she'd not had an easy life. When they were seated in the living room of the main house, he and Keion watched her pace the room. This was going to be bad, he knew it.

Chapter 5

Jacob had spoken to his lady wife about their daughters-in-law and the men, monsters really, that wanted to kill the witches that had been as much a part of the earth as the dragons had. She had explained a great deal to him.

He'd known there were fanatics out there, men and women, who would rather destroy than to understand. It mattered little if it was good or bad; if it didn't conform to whatever idea they had in their head, then they would get rid of it. Murder usually, or simply destroying the very foundations that they used. He'd seen a smaller version of that growing up. Men wanting sons and turning out their daughters and wives when none were born to them. Stupid people.

"My mother was at the stake when she met the king and queen. I know that her version of the events is much different than what really happened. Even Rohm Herald, the man who the group calling themselves the Heralds is named for, had something different in his telling as well. But Caroline was there. I found out later that nearly half the people there were also witches, looking like men so as not to be found out. They were coming to see if they could help her when the time came." Jacob turned to the lovely witch Caroline when she entered the room. "Caroline, you should tell them what really happened that night. And whatever information you might have about what happened before and after. Like how Michael Herald really died."

Caroline was older than him. He thought for sure she might have been around when his king and queen had been born. Of course he'd never ask her, but she had a way about her that made one think old world. And what surprised him most of all was that she wasn't jaded in her age. She took things in stride as if she were a young person. He thought he liked that the most about her. But she wasn't one to trifle with. Her temper was slow to burn; she took her time in getting angry. But once it was unleashed, it was a fury that would fell armies. He'd seen her do that only the one time, and it had been more than enough for him.

"I was there, yes. I knew part of the plan that Anthony and Eve had come up with, not all as it didn't involve me, and we were warned not to interfere with the lives of the others. I had told my king that morning that Mary was in trouble, that her babe too would be killed when she was murdered. I knew not of the second child; I don't think anyone did but the two of them. It was the beginning, I think; of them getting things set for their children. Anyway, the queen had not yet delivered her children by then, I think now, but took a chance to go and see Mary that night to help the unborn child." Caroline sat down next to him and held his hand as she finished. Jacob knew that this was hard on her, remembering things that were better left untold. But she'd do it for them. "They offered Mary a better life, for her child and herself." Shane asked about Lelani. "They knew I'm sure, as I said. The two of them would not have told Mary, thinking her to want double what they were offering. But they knew that there would be twins born of Mary. It wouldn't have hurt them to give her more, but I believe they thought it safer for the child for it to be a secret. My lady queen knew also that Mary would take it wrong and think, as everyone did, that the firstborn would be given all the powers that she gave the child. It had been that way for centuries when a man had a son of his own, no matter how many female children were born to him first. However, what she didn't know, nor care to understand, was that Lelani had her own powers before she was born, and that Erin, the firstborn, got very little from her mother. My lady queen gave Lelani some magic, a few things to help her survive her childhood, but she was born with all that she has even now. Other than long life that she gave to Mary and her, Erin never was much of a witch. Lelani, she was born with immortality."

"My mother was an herbal witch. Her powers weren't that strong, as Caroline said, but she had them. She could mix some herbs, cure some infections, and when she was lucky help a woman through some difficult childbirth pangs. There wasn't really any true magic. But she made out that she was this great and powerful witch, telling everyone, as she had

Rohm, that she could control events and elements. My mother could mix a nice smokescreen when necessary too, but not anything like she claimed she could." Lelani sat down again. "After she was gone, it was easy enough to find out what she'd said, who she had lied to and promised things that she'd never have delivered should she have lived. Rohm believed that my mother had tricked his son into having sex with her when it was consensual between them. Michael's own wife believed what he told her, going so far as to have one of their servants beat a woman to death when she came to tell her of a child. But she soon began to think that there were too many with claims, and they did look like her husband's true children as well. The children—because he also had several bastards in addition to my sister and me—were paid no more support than he did his own children when they needed him. When his wife found out about my mother and the child, she told him she'd quit him if he didn't have her gotten rid of. When he did nothing, she went to her father-in-law and demanded that he take care of the lying woman."

Jacob wondered how a person could simply ignore their responsibilities to a child. How could anyone just abandon them when they helped create them? His own lady wife had no answer for that either when he'd posed the question to her earlier. He listened as Lelani continued.

"When Erin and I were born, there wasn't much in the way of celebrations, I was told. Mother had no money despite the king making sure that she was paid monthly, as was the staff there. And as she had no friends anyway, there would have been few that would have come should she have had a celebration. Mother would borrow, yet never repay, from

104

the very people that were to protect us. Even steal when Erin expressed a desire for something that was well out of their price range." She laughed then, bitterly and sad. "From the first I knew that I was different than my sister. While she was given nearly everything she wanted, even if Mother had to kill to get it, I was left on my own. The king and queen were gone by then. There was no one I could turn to, so the staff and their children got me through my younger years. One of the boys taught me to ride like a man. Another showed me how to use a bow and arrow. I was taught to fight, to use a sword. To spit and curse. By the time that my mother got it in her head that nothing would ever harm us, I had distanced myself from her and Erin a great deal. It would be days, sometimes weeks, before I would return home, only to find that they hadn't noticed or cared. Then it was either leave the area that I'd grown up in or be taken down with Erin when she got it in her head that she was going to work whatever magic she had to in order to be the richest woman alive."

"Your mother would come to watch us in the yard." Lelani nodded at him, and Jacob felt his face heat up. "I'm sorry. I should have taken care to watch over them, I guess, but I never got the impression that it would do me any good. I never knew that there were two of you, daughters I mean. We only saw the one child, and until now, never knew what had happened to either your mother or sister. I knew, of course, that she had died, but not any details about her death. And I even heard about Rohm and his family of affairs. But as we were safe here, upon our own grounds, we didn't bother much with the outside world that was right around us. We did leave out treats at first, extra food for your family, only to go back and find that it had been destroyed, the food thrown around as if it wasn't good enough for them."

"To them, it more than likely wasn't. Nothing was ever good enough unless it was expensive or approved of by Erin. Mom had decided that the king and queen had blessed them in singling out her and her Erin, and I think it went to her head. I know that it did my sister's. She was going to be great, the one that would bring down the people that had killed them, they both thought. But Erin could barely fashion a spell to make the garden grow better, much less take on a job such as finding the people who had killed the king." Lelani sat down again now and held on to her mates' hands. Jacob could see that they loved her, and he loved her all the more for being there. "They're all dead now, their line dried up not long after the castle came down. There are so few of the bloodline left that was there that night that it's doubtful that they'd be able to trace their line back to their ancestors at all. I had nothing to do with it. I think that a curse was put upon those that came to the castle with ill will, and they all just simply stopped producing children. It was a good one, I think. No one can lay claims on things that you might have found here."

Kiaran cleared his throat, and they all looked at him when he spoke. "Your mother was eventually killed, and as much as it pains me to tell you this, your sister was the cause of it. Erin has it in her memories, how she had gone to one of the members of the newly formed Herald and told them that Mary frequented an area off the land that was theirs. Erin had it in her head that she'd be the queen of the household if her mother was gone. To her, you were never a threat. So when your mother ventured too far from the house and the protection there, men were waiting for her and took her to the grounds used to murder innocent women. I don't, however, know what happened to your sister other than she reached out to me and asked me to take her being." Jacob watched Lelani when Kiaran spoke, and he could see the heartbreak on her face. "You never got to look at her memories. Whenever you wish, I'm there for you."

"I think I have my answer now. But should you like to have those memories taken out, I can do that for you. You were never meant to hold them forever, I don't think. Though knowing my sister, she more than likely thought that you'd find her murderer and avenge her death. Perhaps she thought you'd bring her back from the dead as well." It wasn't funny, and the laughter that spilled from Lelani's lips wasn't filled with humor either. She was hurt by this…her sister, her death, the way she had been treated. Jacob could only hope that she was feeling the love that they had for her, and that she'd know that she was their family as well. "I guess, even after all this time, I don't understand. Not why she hated me. Why Mother never thought of me like she did my sister. And until recently, I never understood why a king and queen would care about a low level witch and her unborn bastards. But in order to complete their circle, one to protect their children, they touched the lives of a great many people to make sure that they were safe beyond what they could do for them in life. They made sure that their own children and those of Sally and Jacob were happy and safe. More than most people do for their own children even when they're there with them."

Caroline stood up then and moved to Kiaran as she spoke to the newest member of his family. "I cannot remove them, but I can tell you of her last moments should you like that." Lelani nodded, then shook her head. "It might answer questions that you have buzzing about your head. I know that I have a few of my own."

"I was always wondering why she hated me so much. I guess it matters little now, even after all this time. I tried to help her, to even like her, but she wasn't.... I guess it was my mom's fault. She fed Erin all kinds of things that she believed. Like as the chosen one, she was destined for greatness. Or at the very least to become this great witch. I think she felt that I was beneath them, being second born, and neither the king nor queen acknowledging me."

"But they did. I mean, they knew something about you, but I'm not sure how much. But knowing them, they knew it all." Jacob asked Onimia what he meant. "I found something a few weeks ago when I was talking to Mom and Dad. I had no idea what it was then. I actually thought it might belong to my own mate, and how cool it was to know her name before she got here. But I'd forgotten about it until now. Let me go get it."

"May I?" Caroline got permission to touch Kiaran's head and closed her eyes. "She was hurt before the shot that took her life. Shot with silver. I had no idea that she was wolf too."

"Yes, she thought it would make her a cooler witch if she could shift into an animal. I have no idea why she thought that; her mind worked on a different level than most people's." Jacob thought that was the silliest thing he'd ever heard, to think that being able to shift would make you smarter. "Do you know why she gave her powers to Kiaran and not some other witch?"

"She reached out to the strongest person she could find, thinking that they'd need to be strong to take on her powers. She actually thought of contacting you to give you all that she was, but thought that you would waste them or flitter them away. She also didn't want you to be more powerful than her should she vent all that she had. Vent?" Lelani explained. "She didn't even know that it's called liberating? This girl should have been taken to task long before this. But I digress. She reached for the strongest being she could find. And it just happened to be Kiaran."

"That sounds about like her. Did she know who was trying to murder her? Was it the Herald?" Caroline nodded at Lelani's question and touched Kiaran's head again, and told them that it was one of the Herald group. "It figures. By the way, I talked to one of the descendants this morning. Shook him up a bit too while I was at it."

~~~

Asher was pissed. He really wasn't sure why he was, but he could feel it burning over his body like a well-worn blanket. Christ, what was she thinking? She wasn't, was what his mind kept telling him. She'd talked to the very people trying to kill them.

"You should see your face right now." He glared at Lindsey when she laughed at him. "You might want to take it down a couple of notches there, buddy. I'm not sleeping well as yet, and I can and will call on someone to hurt you."

"The dragons won't hurt me because they know that I'm

their king." She just cocked a brow at him, and he realized how arrogant that sounded. "What I mean is, you'll have to find someone else to do your bidding…the dragons won't touch me."

"Yeah? Maybe so. But do you think that's all that I can call on? Did you know that faeries and brownies will do whatever I tell them? You should remember that." He shifted his daughter in his arms when she fussed at him. For some reason Asher thought little Sally Anne knew that he was being bested by her aunt and thought him foolish. He looked over at Essie to see if there was going to be help there, and Lindsey handed him her little girl and stood up. "I need to stretch for a moment. And to walk. Will you watch her for me? I'll only be a moment."

All thoughts of anger and brownies left his head. The little girls, born on the same day just moments apart, looked up at him. His daughter, named for his mom, Sally Anne, yawned, then stared at him as if to ask him why all the bother. Eve Marie, Jed's little girl, just looked at him with pursed lips. She looked so much like her mother he wanted to laugh. Instead, he thought about why he was angry. And speaking to Lelani in a calm voice so as not to piss her or the girls off, he put a smile on his face so she could hear he wasn't upset any longer.

"Please, the next time you do something like this, whether you're there or not, I'd like it if you were to let one of us know. That way, should it come to it, we can help you. I'm not sure how we could, but we might." Asher looked up at her and she nodded once. "Thank you."

His dad came to sit by him then and took Eve from him. He'd never seen his dad as happy as he was lately. As he held his granddaughter, Dad told her all about her grandma and how much she wanted to see them. When he asked when they could take them, Asher stood up.

"Now. We should take them there now." The message, the one that was brought to them in the form of a mate, ran through his head. The love of Sally would bring forth the love of a mother. As they made their way there, his heart pounding in his chest, all he could think about was his mom.

"It might not work." He looked over at Jed when he spoke. "It's all I thought about too, that love would bring forth a mother since we found out that we were having a baby. You're thinking, as I have, that maybe one of the girls will wake Mom up. I want that to work in the worst kind of way."

"I do too. I guess...I guess with Dad here, all I can think about is Mom being here as well. She'd love all this going on. And I can see her now with the babies, can't you?" Jed nodded and looked ahead. Asher was hesitant now to see if it would work. He knew, deep in his heart, that it wouldn't. "We can only see. And if nothing else, she'll be able to be near them for a time. Right?"

As they all gathered around the small cemetery, he looked at his dad's stone that was covered by a worn tattered quilt. It had been carved, as his mother's had, from the very castle walls. When they'd passed on, it had only seemed fitting that they have a part of it marking their passing. Their lives had been the biggest part of it, the people there bringing them together to create them. He thought of the other graves, ones not far from here, and decided that they should go there as well. See the king and queen and take the babes.

111

His dad had taken Sally Anne this time. And when he sat near the grave of his one true love, Asher and the others stepped back when Lindsey handed Eve to his dad as well. He had no idea, but he thought that Dad should introduce them to their grandmother, and apparently the others did as well. Listening to him now, Asher felt his heart twist in his chest as he pulled Essie to him. His dad really had loved their mom.

"Here they are. Did I not tell you that they were the most beautiful creatures on this earth?" Dad laughed, his head cocked to the side as if listening to some unheard voice. "Yes, I know that you told me all along that they'd be beautiful. But to see them now, it's hard to imagine that we helped in a way to create them. They're so tiny, Sally mine, that I sometimes think I'm to break one of them. You'd be in your glory to see them."

Asher thought again of his mom. She'd been so wonderful. They'd never wanted for anything growing up. She was there for them, teaching them to read and write. There wasn't a time in his life that he ever saw her without a book in her hands when everything was done for the day. Or a blanket she was putting together out of their old clothing. He remembered asking her once why she made so many blankets.

"I won't be around forever, you know. I'm going to live a good long time, yes that's true, but unlike you boys, I'm not an immortal. I can get sick and die." Even then Asher had a feeling that she knew not just that she was surely going to leave them, but the date and time too. "You boys, you grow so much. What should I be doing with all these scraps of material but to keep you warm at night?"

He'd watched out for her for several days after that, having a feeling that she was as close to death as anyone could be. But finally she told him to leave her be, that she'd be there until he was ready to leave on his own. After that, he couldn't remember thinking about it again until she'd gotten sick.

She and Dad had been out picking berries. It was their time, they'd told them, to be by themselves as a couple. He'd never understood that until he was older and a little less full of himself, why anyone would not want to spend time with him.

Asher had been nearly three hundred by that time, bored with life and getting antsy to get out on his own. The rules that they'd learned, all the ones that would keep their family safe, had been there, and he'd never had any idea to ever not keep his family safe. But the need to get out on his own was making him itchy. Then Mom had come back from their outing and he could see that she was ill.

"I'll be all right now. You just go on now and set the table." He hadn't wanted her to make dinner, insisting instead that they all do it. "And what will we be having then? Pork chops again? Those too greasy potatoes? I'm fine, Asher. Go on now and do as I said, please."

She'd taken to her bed about three days later. Dad never left her side, even laying down himself when he'd been beyond exhausted. Asher and the others had taken turns being with them, his dad falling ill too. He knew that it was time; his parents had lived their lives and they wanted to rest.

His mom had taken his hand one morning, the morning that she had passed, and smiled at him. She just held his much larger one in her small worn one. When he kissed the back of it, careful of not hurting her, she smiled at him more brightly. Dad was asleep, and Asher was glad for those few moments alone with his mom.

"I'm ready." His heart broke and he couldn't even tell her he wasn't. "You're a good man, Asher. Better than I hoped for all my life for a son. All my boys, all of you, a mother could not have asked for anything better. But I'm tired and old. Very old, as a matter of fact, and I'm ready to rest. You'll be fine, trust me, Asher. You're going to be just fine."

"I don't want you to leave me." She smiled again, closing her eyes. "Mom, I can't let you go. I need you in my life now more than ever. Please, just stay with us a little longer. Until we're ready."

"You'll be fine." Her breaths were slower then, her body closing down, turning off so that she could go in peace. "Someday you'll meet a woman and she'll knock you on the bottom that I never once had to switch. That's quite an accomplishment when you think of all the trouble you've been in."

He laughed, the sound bursting from him so surprisingly that he kissed her again. Asher had never considered himself a momma's boy, but he knew then that he had been. When she coughed once, he moved closer to her to hear her words.

"I've talked to the others, told them that I love them. I'm so glad that you're here for your father." Yes, he said, he was glad as well, but he'd be happier with her there. "He'll join me soon. His heart and mine are forever tied to each other. You'll have that as well. But I don't want you to mourn us, Asher. Life, our life, was full, so full that I wondered at times

114

how I'd been so lucky. I love you, son. With all my heart."

His dad woke then, just sat up in the bed and pulled Mom to him. And when she took her last breath, Dad had held her, tears flowing unchecked down his face. Four days later, his dad's heart broken, as he told Asher, he went to bed, the same one that he'd shared with his wife, and didn't wake. Asher had left home soon after, too many memories for him to feel happy there any longer. But he came back and found his own love, his own life, and now had a little girl too.

Asher looked around. He knew this land like he did the back of his hand...the castle grounds as well. As he stood there, holding Essie as his dad talked to their mom, he saw the tree he'd fallen out of as a young child. The creek bank that he'd caught his first fish from. The apple tree and other fruit trees he'd helped pick from for his mom to make jams and jellies. He thought that there was no better place in the world to have a family than right here.

"We should visit the king and queen. Take the babies to see them as well. No one can hear them, so I'm not sure they can communicate with us, but I'd like to do that." He told Gideon that he'd thought that as well. "I can't wait for you to see the tomb room that we built for them. Onimia and I worked hard on it, and it's finished now."

"I'm sure that it's perfect. You had a plan and I'm sure you stuck to it. That's one of the many wonderful things about you, Gideon...you think things out completely better than anyone I know." He did have many qualities that the rest of them didn't. The drawings had been made weeks ago, just after it was decided that the couple should be near where

115

their children had been safe. Parts of the castle would be used, he'd told them, as well as some of the items they'd unearthed at the site. And after drawing names to see who would decide where the resting place was — Gideon and Onimia winning the draw — it was decided that it would be a surprise for them as well.

The mountain was as giving to them as the soil was as they made their way to the tomb. Lights lined the path to the lower levels of the cave, and the further down they went, Asher could see that they'd taken their time there as well. There were benches along the way, rocks with deep crevices in them that were filled with gems and stones that lit up when they were close to them. And when they reached the room, a place so extraordinary to them all, Asher could only stare. It was far better than he'd thought it would be. He hugged Gideon when he asked him how he liked it.

"Just as I had thought it would be. Beautiful, and so peaceful here. There is nothing at all that I'd change, and I'm sure the others think so as well." Asher looked around more and saw all the small touches that they'd brought to the place, and was prouder in that moment than he'd ever been.

The bodies of both the king and the queen were laid on a large stone. Asher would bet that it was the same stone that had felled the king that night. They lay side by side, their hands just touching. One of Asher's mother's own blankets covered their bodies, as if they'd only laid there to rest. Some of the treasures that they'd found when excavating the castle were there too, lain about the room and on the dais, and Asher walked closer so he could see them better.

A bit of lace that had been unearthed was over her face.

A gem that had a dragon carved into its surface lay upon the king's heart. A bracelet that had been found, which Daniel had said was his sister's, was now encircling the queen's wrist. The sword that they'd found beside the body of the king lay at his side, and the knives that had been with the body of the queen were at hers. They were as beautiful in death as he'd bet they had been in life.

Around the room there were other such things. Two place settings of the pattern that they'd been told was picked by them. A basket, ill formed and not well made, was there too. One of the smaller dragons had told them that the queen had tried to help one day, and that was what she got for her efforts. The year had been carved in a small flat stone and put beside it.

Asher walked more around the room and saw that there was a stone at the foot of the dais that had both their names on it, a pair of dragons, as well as the year that they had died. Beneath the date, their names had been inscribed, and the year that they'd been born as well. He ran his finger over the names of his family, including the dragons that were as much his brothers as the others were.

There were pieces of tapestry, bits of cloth framed and set upon a stone shelf. Some other items, like a hair brush and a trencher that they'd found, were there as well. All the parts, all the pieces of their life, lay around the couple that had given them as much life as their own parents had.

"What do you think?" He looked over at his brother and wondered why he'd even ask. "You have the strangest look on your face. I can't tell if you're angry, shocked, or pleased."

"Not angry. Pleased? Yes, very much so. Shocked? Oh yes. I don't think I thought about what you'd do, but knew that you'd do very well. But surely even you're surprised as to how well it turned out." Gideon smiled, then nodded. "You did something very wonderful here. And for generations now, we can come here and talk to them in both comfort and peace. And our children, as well as theirs, can come here to talk to the people who made it all possible for us."

"Thank you, Asher. Coming from you, that means so much more to me. We had hoped that you'd like it, maybe even be a little in awe of us, but your words, they have special meaning because I know that they come from your heart." He hugged his brother again. "Now, let's show off those beautiful baby girls. By the way, have you thought of their own mates? And what they're going to be like?"

Asher was still standing there with his mouth open when Essie pushed it closed. She was looking at him like she wasn't sure if he was her mate or not. Taking Sally Anne from her, he glared at no one in particular and held his daughter close.

"She is not going to find a mate. And she will not leave our home without an escort. If I must, I will put magic all around her to keep all males away." She just looked at him, then laughed. "I'm serious. No one is going to touch my little girl."

"Whatever you say, Asher. I'm sure you can make that happen."

He had a feeling she was still laughing at him as they made their way back to the house. He'd just see about this whole dating and finding a mate thing. This was his baby girl. No one was going to.... Well, no one was going to do anything to her.

Chapter 6

Robert stood before his congregation and thought of how proud Rohm would be right now. They were seventy members strong and getting stronger every day. When one of the men stood and asked to bring something before the group, Robert sat in his chair.

The group was composed of all men, and he could see the reason for the first group being that way as well. Men were less inclined to be emotional, out of sorts for no reason. And they would not insist that the food they were having be healthy and nutritious as his own wife had done before he left to come here tonight. Robert was growing tired of his wife's ways, and needed to think on how to rid himself of the ball and chain she was fast becoming. Running his hand down along the arms of his chair, he had to smile. It was perfect for the head of this clan. Perfect.

And it was a monstrosity. Too big for even the size of the room they were in. But he had fallen in love with it when he'd come across it at an estate sale, paying the asking price when he knew he could get it cheaper if he were to haggle. Robert had to go without lunch for an entire month just to pay for it so that his first wife wouldn't see it.

Lynne hadn't liked it any better when he'd shown it to her, and insisted that he take it out of the house. He was beginning to hate to take things into his own home, knowing that she was going to make him take it right back out again. That was added to his mental list of things that Lynne was doing to piss him off. Robert really was going to have to do something about—

"I have a problem with my wife's mother. I'm thinking that she might be a witch." Robert wanted to tell him that mothers-in-law, by their very nature, were all witches, but waited as the rest of the group asked him what she'd done to him. "Just last night she came to our house and told my wife that she needs to make me find a job. I had to put my foot down on that one. I do have a job, and she has no right telling me what to do. I might be only making a little money here working the phones, but it's a job and she don't have any right to tell me it's not."

"How does that make her a witch?" It was a good question, and Robert was curious to see how the man answered the question put to him. "And while we're at it, I'm thinking my wife might be as well. She sure did put a hex on my cock. And now I'm not able to perform at all. Not even my mistress can get me up."

Robert only marginally believed in magic. He knew that

there were ways to combine herbs, chemicals, and other things to get effects that would certainly look magical. Like he'd seen a trick that his son had done in preschool that was labeled as magic. He'd put a daisy in a glass of blue water and it turned the flower petals blue, thus draining all the color from the water. He had been so thrilled with the results that he'd tried the same thing on everything in the house. The dog had had his tail dunked in the bathtub so much that he'd run away some months ago, never to return.

As the conversation went on around him, each man telling how they thought their own wife or someone that they knew were witches, Robert thought of his own wife. Not Lynne, who was beginning to wear on his nerves, but Beth, his first wife. She'd not been a witch, but a pain in his ass for sure.

He'd killed her and her father when she told him that she was filing for a divorce. Beth had come from money, a great deal of it, and when she'd agreed to marry him, Robert really had loved her. Or so he thought. It was the things that her money could bring to him and his causes that he truly loved. And even then he had a great many causes that he enjoyed. The cause to get him laid more. The cause to get him a new boat and new clothing. All things that he'd loved about having money at his fingertips at any time. Like the new house, the cars he would get carted around in, as well as new suits when he found a small spot on an old one. Money had made his world perfect.

"Where is the money?" He asked her what she was talking about when she dared question him as soon as he walked in the door. Her father was there again; he'd laughed when

123

Beth had told him she wanted to speak to him before dinner. Robert still believed that Pete had a lot do to with her asking questions after all this time. When they were in his office and she was seated at his desk, all he could think about was the woman's bed he'd just left and the hangover he was having. "I talked to the bank today. They said that you've gone through nearly forty thousand dollars this month alone. What are you spending it on, Robert? We have everything we need here."

"You have everything you need, not me. I have a business to run. And other partnerships that you'd not understand. By the way, how long is your father going to be staying this time? You know how much I hate him being here. He's always in my business. And so you know, I'm not going to functions with the two of you. I have things going on right now." She pulled out his book, the one that had been in his family for generations. "What the hell are you doing with that? I've told you over and over to stay out of my things. Am I going to have to start locking things up from you from now on, Beth? Not very trusting, are you?"

"Trust? You don't have the slightest clue what that word even means. But this? You're trying to get this joke of a group back up and going, aren't you? You know as well as I that there are no witches, there is no magic. What you're doing is foolishness, and I'll not have it." He started to tell her that she'd do as she was told when she continued. "You'll not have any more disposable money at your beck and call. As of now, your credit cards no longer work. I'll not have you putting my family in the poor house."

"*You'll* not have it? I wasn't aware that at some point you became my mother. Or had the rights to tell me what

I can and can't do. Fuck you, Beth. I'll do as I damned well please." The fights between them had grown more vicious, as well as violent. He'd hit her more than once over the last few months, and his hand was burning to do so now. "Shall I remind you again that I'm the man of this house? You'd like that, wouldn't you…to be able to run to daddy dearest and have him threaten me again."

"I'm filing for divorce." He started to tell her that she was not when she spoke again. "Dad is going to help me. And because of the prenup that you signed when we married, you won't get another dime from me. Or my estate."

"You can't divorce me. I won't have it." She laughed at him and he did hit her then. Knocked her back into the credenza behind her, knocking the pictures there over onto their faces. When she didn't move, he'd thought for sure that he'd killed her. And when her father came rushing into the room, telling him to get out, he'd done the only thing he could do and had pulled his gun out and killed them both.

It only took him a moment to realize that he had fucked up. And a few more for him to think of a plan. The staff wasn't in residence that day, it being Wednesday, so he knew that no one would have heard the noise. Going to the phone, he called Lynne and asked her if he could come over to talk to her, telling her that his father-in-law was in the house and he'd needed a place to stay.

Then he'd left the front door open and left the house. The next morning it had been all over the news that someone had killed Beth Herald and her father, Peter Winebarger, in cold blood. His alibi, a crappy one to say the least, sleeping over at his girlfriend's house, had given him all he needed to not get caught. But then no one had been caught, so he wasn't sure where he stood on that one either.

He and Lynne had married not long after he'd gotten his money from both estates. It was both a pleasant surprise and a great windfall to have known that he was the only living heir to his father-in-law's estate, too. Since he'd left all his worldly goods to his only child, Robert's wife, he had gotten that as well. But it didn't last as long as he'd hoped. Not nearly long enough for him to have as much fun as he'd thought they would with it. Then Lynne had gotten knocked up and he'd been even poorer. And just a bit ago, about three months now, he'd lost his job because he'd been spending more time at his hobby, as Lynne called it, than actually working. But he was going for greatness.

When he thought of spending forty million dollars in ten years without a thing to show for it, he got depressed. And when he was depressed, Robert went looking for women he could take his depression out on. A few good punches to the face, a fast fuck against the wall, and he was good to go. Until the next time. Robert smiled, thinking that his *depression* was certainly convenient to his dick getting used.

And he was no closer to recouping his money than he had been the day that the bank had told him he was broke. So broke, in fact, that he'd had to sell the house that had been in Beth's family for ten generations, the cars that he didn't drive because some fool had purchased stick shifts and not automatics, and the book collection that he'd not even known existed until then.

The men that had joined him in the Herald were to pay

him dues each month. So far he'd only collected about half of what they owed him; some of the men were poorer than him, it seemed. But he would hound them, just enough, until they finally paid up or stopped coming to the meetings altogether. Today he had a list of the ones that were way behind in their billing, and he was going to have a long talk with them. He needed to buy his pretty little mistress a bauble for taking his shitty mood out on her last night.

Robert looked up from his list when he realized that the room had grown incredibly quiet.

"So? Can we?" He had no idea what had been discussed, so he looked around the room for some hint. "We can do like that book of yours says. If they manage to get out of the flames, then we know that they're really witches and we are well within our rights to kill them. If not, well, we were wrong, but we'll know better next time."

"You wish to burn someone at the stake?" The man nodded, the wobble under his chin going faster than his bobbing head did. "You mean to bring a woman out to the land and have her burned at the stake like you're grilling out? You do know what sort of mess that'll make...the smell. Why don't you just kill her?"

"I'm sure it will be unpleasant, but that's the only way to kill a witch. And if she's not then it would be murder. Not that we care. But we need to do this correctly. I mean, Christ, you should have heard all the things I tried to get rid of her before this." Robert was beginning to see the merit to this way of getting rid of the wives. No alimony, no child support, both of which he'd be stuck with should he divorce Lynne. Most of the men's spouses, according to the stories from the others, were just as bad if not worse than his own wife. "We have all decided that we'd be better off getting this nipped in the bud rather than waiting until they murder us with their magic."

He told him he'd have to think about it. And as they filed out, he was handed a sheet of paper from each of them, all of them stating that they would take to the grave what was said here tonight. Also, there were notes on the things that had made them think that their wives were witches. Some of them were pretty scary.

Picking up the phone, he tried to call Cybil again. Over the last few days he'd called at least a dozen times and had left her six or seven messages. He thought now and then of what Lelani had said to him, that Cybil would be of no more help, but there was no way that this woman had gotten the jump on a witch like Cybil. Robert needed to know if there were indeed dragons on the land where she was staying. And if so, how that was possible. But he couldn't contact her, and wondered if Lelani had killed her like she'd said. Hanging up, he dialed the number of the other witch that he had on his limited payroll. She answered on the second ring.

"I'm quitting you. The last two checks from you bounced, and I have needs." He told her he'd call the bank first thing. "You do that. But I'm still done with you. Besides, I'm thinking it was a mistake to help you out. There are things going on here that scare the shit out of me."

"What sort of things? Dragons?" He knew when she didn't answer him that she'd seen them. "How big are they? What do they look like?"

"So many that they blacken the sky when they fly

overhead. Their fire warms the ground so that not even the frost bothers the flowers and trees." She laughed then, her voice tight with the fear he was beginning to feel. "I'm not going to stay here. I have a feeling that I'd be better off out there where your minions can find me rather than trying to make it in this place. The things that they could do to me here would be worse than anything you can make up out there."

"Get me a picture of one of them. You do that and I'll make sure that you're free of the Herald for the rest of your days, as well as your children and their children." He wouldn't do that, of course. She was on the list of known witches, and the first time one of them saw her, she'd be dead. Just as Erin Wayne had been. "You do that and I promise you more riches than you can ever imagine."

"You don't have any more money than I do. If you did, then my check wouldn't be bouncing around like one of them balls in a big house." She had a point. "But I'll do this, take a picture of one of them. But not for you. I'm going to sell it to the highest bidder and be—"

He heard the shuffle, and the scream that accompanied it was cut off abruptly. Gripping the phone tightly to his ear, he tried to hear what had happened to the person at the other end when he heard laughter. Laughter that he'd heard before. As he started to hang up, he heard her tisking at him.

"Now why would you not at least ask me what was done to her? That's sort of rude, when you know as well as I that you're burning…well, not burning, I guess. You have that plan for your own wife, don't you? And after all that she's done for you." He closed his eyes and willed her to not be real. "Oh, I'm real all right. And you'd do well to remember that, Robert. And so you know, I'm coming for you too."

~~~

Lelani fingered the large bracelet. Her name, spelled out in the most perfect gems she'd ever seen, seemed to just reach out to capture the light and sparkle it back to her. The clasp, made of gold, she thought, was topped with the biggest opal she'd ever seen. Onimia had found it one day, thinking to save it for his own mate. He'd given it to her just that morning.

She looked up when Shane said her name.

"Do you not like it?" Telling him she did, Lelani leaned back in her seat and told him that she'd gone to see Rachel. "The other witch that was selling us out."

"Yes, that's her. I'm sorry, but she's gone." He just nodded. "Did you hear what I said? I killed her. Of course, I only went there to talk to her, to see if we could work something out, but she used her magic against me, and had it not been for Roger, she would have hurt me badly."

"Then I'm glad that you took defensive actions. I'd rather you were never hurt again. Now, I wanted to talk to you about your magic and what you think we've gotten from you." Lelani just stared at him. "Do you think we can do that visit thing you do?"

"Visit thing? You mean teleport yourself as an image elsewhere? I'm not sure. Why do you want to?" He explained. "You think that'll work? I mean, it would so long as no one tried to touch you. But why would you not want to go and conduct business in person? I mean, you don't seem to mind people the way that I do."

"I love people, usually. But if I can be there and not have

130

to leave here, then I'd be happier. The thought of not being with you would make me nuts." She thought it was time she told them she needed space, a little anyway. But he continued before she could. "Also, Keion and I were talking and we realized that we're taking up a great deal of your time. I mean, if we're not making love to you, we're thinking about it. I think you had a job before us, didn't you?"

"Yes. I repaired paintings and tapestries. Why did you think that I'd want to leave here anymore than you would? I don't, but why did you think of that?" He leaned back in his seat and smiled. "Charming as you are, that is not an answer. I want you to tell me why you want me to work."

"I don't. I mean, if you want to, then that's wonderful. If you'd rather just putter around the house and yard, Keion and I are all right with that as well." Lelani told him he was making no sense. "I know, and I'm sorry. What I meant to say is, we have more than enough money if that is the issue. If you want to try a new thing—I have no idea what that would be— then that's great as well. What I'm trying to tell you in my fuddled way is, whatever makes you happy makes us happy as well."

"I have money. A great.... Have you tried to look into the future?" He asked her what she meant. "I got this thing from the king and queen. I'm pretty sure that's where it came from. Anyway, I can see into the future. Pretty far too. I can't see yours or Keion's, nor can I see my own, not really, but I can see that Asher, Kiaran, and Essie have six more children. Three more girls and three little boys. Jed, Casdon, and Lindsey have one more child, because they find that adopting children

131

that are orphaned because of something in their DNA makes the world a better place for them. They want children that the parents don't understand or don't care to that are magical. What I was getting to was that I can see where things are going in the world of inventions. I've invested in things that seemed farfetched at the start, yet have become a household name. Perhaps you can do the same."

"And you profited from them. That's great." She told him that she donated a great deal of it to causes. "You do that because you can't profit from your magic. I forgot about that. Ariannona told us that to take and take will come back to bite you in the ass. You're supposed to give ten times what you borrow, right?"

"I can so long as a lot of the money or whatever goes not to me but to help others. Yes, I must give back ten times what I use in magic." He asked her like what. "New burn units at hospitals. Children services. College funds for people that need it. There are a great many ways to help others without anyone ever knowing who their benefactor is. And while I don't care for people as a whole, there are some pretty good ones and I help them when I can. They don't have to take it, but it's there for them."

"You're a very generous and wonderful person." She told him she really wasn't. "I think you are, and that's all that matters. Keion thinks you're the greatest. I have to agree with him there. You're pretty special. But before I get sidetracked again by stripping you down to that lovely bare skin of yours, tell me what happened with the witch, and I'm assuming Robert James."

She had told them what she'd been able to find out about

the man who was in charge of the fanatical group that was out to kill all witches. But today she'd found out a little more. This was scarier than just them hunting witches and killing them.

"They have it in their heads, this group of men that follow him, that they're able to kill anyone that they deem unworthy. Such as one man wishes to kill his neighbor's husband so that the wife will let him fuck her when she has the itch. I never really understood that term, but anyway. A couple more of them are going to kill off their own wives; they either have lost their young appeal for them or they just want them gone to pursue women in general. And they have thought that by claiming that they're witches, all of them, then they can be justified in killing the people that they swore to love. I have no idea where they get the idea that the police won't care, but it's not discussed nor figured into their plans." She thanked Roger when he brought her and Shane each a glass of tea, as well as a large tin of scones. He also handed her a sheet of paper; she read it over quickly then handed it to Shane. "A list of all the men in the group. Believe it or not, they have a charter with dues and everything. But according to what I've been able to find out, most of them are behind in their payments. Also, it might interest you to know that Robert was the one that murdered his first wife and her father. The police don't have enough to pull him in, but I'm thinking once his current little wife finds out that he's seeing her replacement, she might recant her story about him being with her all night long."

"What are your plans for him? I'm assuming that you

have one." She nodded. "Is it bad? Am I going to have to take all our money and bail you out of jail for it?"

"No, nothing like that. But I would like go to one of his little meetings…on his turf, but by my rules. And his clan. Show them a force of witchcraft like they've never seen before." He didn't say anything. "Also, the dragons. I think they need to see the dragons as well."

"To what end?" She told him. "You hope to drive him over the edge? I'm assuming you think he's pretty close to that now."

"I'm not sure. There are times when he is close to being as insane as you'd think. But then he has moments of clarity that make me believe that he might be smarter than I thought. My plan, if I can get your permission to do so, is to let him see us in all our glory, then have him bring the police in. I can take care that they see nothing but a family living and making the world work around them. Benson is, after all, a very upstanding family name." He asked her about the dragons. "No one sees them that I don't want to now. I've taken care that they're not seen even when they fly directly overhead unless they need to be. Rachel needed to see them, so that she'd report them to Robert. He, of course, didn't believe her, but I'm thinking he needs a dose of reality to give him enough to get his ass in some serious trouble."

"With the police." She nodded. "You think that in his fear, he'll confess to something? Like the killing of his first wife and father-in-law?"

"Yes." She would explain that to him should he ask, but she hoped that he wouldn't. Robert was going to confess about his killing the other two. But he was going to have a little help from her in doing it.

Lelani knew something that few did. Beth Herald had been pregnant when she'd been killed. Unknown to anyone not magical, as she'd only been a few days into her child's life, he'd taken it when he'd killed his wife. And for that alone, he was going to pay.

"You'll need to bring this up before the family. We would all have to agree to these terms." She had already figured on that and told him so. "Anything else? Do you need to tell me anything pressing at this very moment?"

"No, not that I can think of." He told her to lay back. "What are your plans for me, Shane? I thought that we could only have sex when you were both here."

He paused in reaching for her. "No. There are no rules regarding being with you. Do you only want to have sex with the two of us at the same time? I'm sure if I were to call Keion in, he'd gladly join us."

"I never thought about it until just now, to be honest. I just assumed." He nodded and put his hands up under her blouse, and then her bra. "Will Keion be upset with us? I mean, I don't want either of you upset about us."

"No. He knows that we're here together. And he said that if he were here now and I was out at the castle like he is, then he'd surely take advantage of you." She nodded, still not sure. "We're not jealous of each other, Lelani. We both love you equally, and want whatever makes you happy. If making love to us both at the same time makes you happy, then I can wait."

"What are you going to do to me?" He grinned, and she

felt her body heat with it. "You're too sexy for your own good, you know that, don't you? And so you know, when I go and talk to your family, we're doing that on my terms, not Asher's. I love to shake his world up."

"He knows that too." Shane kissed her bare belly as he moved her pants down along her hips. "I don't want to talk about Asher or any of the other members of the family right now. What I want to do is make love to you."

"Yes."

When he had her pants down and off her, she wanted to beg him to take her now. But she had a feeling that he wanted to do this slowly, take his time and drive her insane. Keion was thorough in his making love to her; Shane was as well, but he was methodical and sometimes bordering on cruel. She had a feeling that she was going to hurt a great deal before he gave her what she needed.

Shane

Chapter 7

Shane loved the taste of her skin, the way her breathing would skip when he nipped at her flesh. The way that she hummed when she was enjoying whatever he was doing to her, and mostly the way that she smelled when aroused. There was nothing about this woman that he disliked. To him, she was perfection.

Swirling his tongue into the small indentation at her belly, he put his hands into the elastic of her panties. He wanted to tear them off her, have her bared for him completely. But he also knew that she came harder when she was teased, and he wanted that more than anything else. To hear her scream out her release with his name on her lips.

When he had them off her, Shane took them to his nose and inhaled deeply. They smelled of her cream, her body, and the lotions that she used when she got out of the shower.

Tossing them over his shoulder, he ran his hands up and down her thighs, listening to her breathing change just a little when he touched her. He enjoyed the way she was panting just as well, the heat of her breath when it touched him.

"When I taste you, eat you, do you have any idea how filling I find that? How much it satisfies me when you come in my mouth?" Lelani moaned and nodded, then shook her head. "Are you going to come for me, love? How hard am I going to have to touch you to bring you over?"

"Very little. Shane, please, give me something. I need you to do something to relieve the pressure." He chuckled a little and moved closer to her open thighs. "I'm going to hurt you if you don't do something."

"No you won't. You love this as much as I do." He blew over her swollen clit peeking just a little from her equally swollen lips. "I'm going to suckle you, drink from you, while you flood me with your juices. Then when I've had my fill, I'm going to take you to the floor and fuck you hard and fast."

"Please." Spreading her nether lips, he blew over her again. When she cried out, her climax taking her, he slid his fingers into her and fucked her while he lapped at her cream. Bringing her twice more, he sat up and took off his shirt. "Take me. Please, just take me."

"Not yet. There is so much of you to explore, and I won't be rushed." He thought she growled at him but he didn't say anything. He was pretty sure that she'd hurt him like she'd threatened if he did. "Would you like for me to come all over your pretty body?"

"Yes. Then fuck me." He stood up and pulled his pants off with his boxers and shoes at the same time. When she sat up, reaching for him, he backed up. "Let me taste you like this."

"No, you'll make me come and I'm not ready yet. Lie back for me. Let me touch you all over first." She did as he requested, but her body was hard with need. He got to his knees beside the couch, holding his cock in his hand. Shane took her nipple into his mouth and suckled hard at just the tip. Her fingers in his hair had him crushing her into his face when she pulled him closer, but he was a man on a mission. And he wasn't going to be hurried.

Untangling her fingers from his hair, he moved down her body, kissing her ribs and licking the tiny freckles as he found them. Tickling her navel brought him such joy that he was surprised when she cursed at him. Looking at her face, he could see that she was indeed in pain.

Sliding his fingers into her pussy again, he thumbed her clit gently as he watched her face. "Come for me, my love; scream the house down with your release."

Her release was beautiful, her voice like a choir of angels singing out his name. And when he buried his mouth over her pussy, never stopping his fingers from playing, she came three more times, each of them more powerful than the one before it. Standing up over her, his cock nearly bursting with his own need, he told her to come to him.

When she was on her feet, a little unsteadily, he picked her up and told her to hold on. As he slammed her down over his cock, he felt his first climax take him. Just like that, he came hard and fast into her. Taking her to the floor—not an easy descent when she was kissing, biting, and touching him everywhere she could — Shane fucked her gently at first, then harder when she wrapped her legs around his hips. Holding her steady, he took her harder than he ever had before.

"Come." She shook her head, telling him that she had no more in her. "Come for me and I'll fill you."

When she bowed up off the floor, her nails digging so deeply into his back that he felt blood, Shane lifted her ass up so that her pussy was tight to his cock and came hard.

He saw stars and dragons, and his body screamed through a second, then a third climax as he took her throat. And when he bit down, tasting her spiked spicy blood sliding down the back of his throat, Shane came a final time and his world simply blinked out.

When he woke he was in the bed. There were no lights on in the room, but he knew that he was alone in the big bed. Laying there, counting his blessings as he did so, he thought of what his life had been before she'd come to him. Rolling to his side, he looked at the box, a very old tin box, that she'd brought into the room her first week with them.

He'd never thought to ask her what was in it. She, of course, never mentioned it either. Shane found that while he was curious as to what it might hold, he also knew that he'd never look without her permission. Lelani was a very private person, and he'd hurt her, he knew, if he did something behind her back. Getting up, he made his way to the shower to get ready to see what the house was doing. He found that he was suddenly hungry as well. The light touch to his mind made him tense up, but when his dad spoke to him, he waited for him to get around whatever bend he was crossing to get to the point. His dad could take more side trips when telling you about something than anyone he ever knew.

There she was, just standing there, and I near had me a heart attack. He asked him who. *Caroline. I was coming out of the barn, didn't even know that we had one, when she was standing right there. I've been scared before, you know. When you were lost that time. Who would have thought that someone could get so far so fast in just minutes? I do hope that the other two are on their toes more than I was. But then those grandbabies of mine are going to be great.*

Dad? What are you talking about? He said he'd just told him. *I didn't get it then. Just start over and tell me why Caroline was at the barn door. If that was the point of the story.*

You're not listening very well. I told you right up, she scared me when she came to tell me that the Herald was calling a meeting. We should have more family meetings, I think. I'm sure that we'd be better – Shane simply said "Dad." *I floated off again, didn't I? But yeah, the Herald is gathering together tonight. Something about a to-do about some witches. Can't see how that's even possible that they might have them one when they're all right here. Speaking of which…no pun there, son, though it was a really good one, don't you think? Anyway, the witch Rachel, have you seen her around?*

She tried to kill Lelani so she had to kill her. His dad said he was glad for that, her making sure she was safe. *Dad, why did you need Rachel?*

Oh, didn't I tell you? Sorry, I got a little sidetracked again. Happens when your mind is so full of things you want to do now that the babies are here. I'm telling you, Shane, I cannot wait for them to start talking to me. He wondered if they'd be as talkative as their grandda, but said nothing. *But her husband called here for her. Just a bit ago. I told him that I'd not seen her, which is true.*

The newer witches, they're more social than the older ones. This Rachel, I think she's not considered really old, not like you and me old, but — He said his name again. *Yeah, well, her husband called and was wondering where she's gone to. He told me that she was supposed to call him nightly so he can be assured that she's safe. I thought spouses were welcome here too. I don't know what I might have done should your momma have been relocated somewhere and me not be able to go with her. I would have missed her something —*

Did he tell you how he knew she might be here? His dad said he'd not thought of that until he'd hung up. *I wonder how he got this number. Or any of our numbers.*

Could be that his wife gave it to him. Hang on, son. That lovely mate of yours is here and I'll talk to her. You come on over to the big house. We got some things going on you need to be working on too. He told him he'd be there in ten minutes even as he stepped under the spray. *Good. Good. I'll try and save you a couple of those scones that Elbert is baking now, but I'm not making you any promises.*

Not only were there plenty of scones left, but there was hot tea and cream to go with them. He sat down next to Lelani and Keion. She was stressing again; being around all of them did that to her. But instead of leaving them, she took both their hands in hers and let out a long breath. Shane squeezed her hand tightly in his and kissed her on the mouth just as Asher stood up to talk to them.

~~~

Keion listened to his brother, wondering not for the first time how his brother had gotten so smart. Yes, Kiaran was a part of Asher, had basically attended the same classes he had in college, read the same books too. But while Kiaran spoke of

142

what he'd found out from a source at the police department and what they might need to do, he wondered what the hell else could go daisy up, as Elbert said all the time.

"Since the death of his first wife and father-in-law, Robert has had someone watching him from the police department. So far they could only get him on a few things, mostly things that would get him a light tap on the wrist and nothing more. But they're wanting him for murder, of the both of them. He looks good for the deaths of Beth and Peter, but they have nothing. He has an airtight alibi. His prints, of course, were all over the house and weapon, but as he lived there and owned the gun, there is little to nothing they can do about it. The police admit that they screwed up a couple of things too." He handed each of them a copy of the report that had been filed back when the murders had happened. "No one bothered to see if he'd fired a gun recently. But it's doubtful that it would have done them much good. Apparently Robert belonged to a gun club that would meet weekly to shoot a few rounds into the targets that were set up. Also, when the girlfriend came forward to say he'd been with her all night, no one had bothered to check on the tapes that had looped around five hundred times by the time it was thought of."

"She was in the process of divorcing him." Shane looked around the room and wondered why no one had thought that was motive enough. But Asher continued before he could ask. "Her father had traveled down from his home, to be there for his daughter apparently, and to have the bastard — that's what he called Robert even to his face — thrown out on his ass. But when he got there, according to the testimony from

Robert himself, the three of them had talked it over and he was simply going to move out for a while. He told the police that he had gone to Lynne's house to tell her that he was going to make his marriage work. I'm guessing that it became a little more than just a talk, and he ended up staying the night. According to the two of them."

"What does he say happened to end up with them both dead?" Asher looked at Lelani and she stood up. "You know what he did?"

"Yes. He hit his wife in the face…he was pissed off and thought that he'd killed her. But before he could confirm whether or not he'd killed her then, Peter came in and started telling him he was going to end him. Robert pulled out his gun—he'd only just gotten it back that day from the shooting range after it was cleaned—and killed first Peter, then Beth." When she started pacing, he knew there had to be more to the story than just that. As he waited, he looked around the room at the rest of them.

Caroline and Gobi had joined them. They were becoming regulars at the dinner table as well when they got together. The babies, both of them doing well, were asleep in the little bassinets that were close to their moms. Keion noticed that each time someone passed the little cribs, they'd reach in and touch them before moving on to whatever task they'd been doing. Even he felt the need to touch their tiny cheeks or hands when they were close by.

Izic was there, along with his mate. There was also Daisy, the dragon that had been staying with Lindsey since she arrived. Essie could be found in the accompaniment of one or two brownies or faeries as well. Shane wondered if Lelani would have one too, and realized that with Roger there, she'd have no need for something magical. When Lelani stopped in front of Kiaran, he watched her carefully.

"The man that killed my sister. You saw him, correct?" Kiaran said that he had. "I would very much like to see him too. And take the memories that you have there, if you don't mind. I think they might help us with this."

"You do what you need to do. I can see them there, even sort through them, but they're not an intrusion." She nodded. "She hated you, yes, but it was more to do with the things that your mother fed her rather than anything you might have done or said to her, as you thought."

"Thank you, that helps a great deal. I think, maybe, she and I might have been at least tolerable to each other had I gone to see her after Mother was killed." She smiled sadly. "Or maybe not. She had Mother murdered. And even with the fact that Mother and I weren't close, it's hard to like someone that kills their own mother, don't you think?"

"I'm sorry, love."

She nodded and asked Kiaran if he was ready. When he nodded, she touched her fingers to his head. When she backed from him seconds later, he thought that something had gone wrong. But when Kiaran thanked her, he realized just how strong she was. In seconds, she'd done what Caroline said that she wasn't able to.

"The man who shot my sister is Robert Herald. His real name is James, as I might have mentioned before, and while he doesn't really believe in any of this, the magic and the dragons, he sees a way to profit by having men follow him.

The dues paid to him, when they're paid, go toward paying his mortgage as well as his cell phone bill. He hasn't worked for months, and the little money that his wife managed to squirrel away is all gone by now as well. Robert is broke." Asher asked about the money that he'd inherited from his first wife. "Gone too. He was living a lifestyle before she died that was well beyond what they could maintain. And once she was gone, he cashed in all her stocks, and there hasn't been any more coming into those accounts. And a few months ago he lost his job, the insurance that went with it, as well as the few perks that he was allowed. His wife — and you should know that he plans to kill her as well — is starting to notice the lack of bills being paid."

"He is now trying to convince someone to cater his party tonight." Izic came into the room speaking and sat next to his mistress, Ariannona. "I was told to watch him, and today he made several calls to see about food being brought in. No one is willing to work with him. Apparently he has not paid any bills from before. I have also helped that along by messing up phone numbers that he is trying to call. A few footprints here and there and a five could be mistaken for an eight. A seven a fat zero."

"Before? You said that he hadn't paid bills from before." Izic nodded at Shane. "You mean that he's called a meeting before to kill someone? Do the police know this?"

"No one was killed, thankfully, at that meeting. Mostly they just sit around drinking and eating and talking about the supposed witches that they come across." Lelani sat down beside him and Shane as she continued. "Tonight, however, there are bigger plans. And Roger has been watching them build a pyre. There are several cords of wood being brought in as well. I have no idea why they'd do this when someone will surely notice the enormous fire they will have. I wonder if they even realize that witches weren't actually burned at the stake in this country."

"It was the threat of it, I think." Keion asked Caroline what she meant. "Women, sometimes even children, were said to have been tainted by black magic when a doctor, mostly a fool who was steady with a knife, couldn't figure out what sort of disease a person might have. Or worse yet, something so common as freckles or red hair. Anything and everything that made them different, not *normal,* as they called it, were subject to tests to see if they were indeed witches. But the stake, or the threat of it, was never used all that often. What they did, however, was just as barbaric. They would hang them, even children, remove their heads, and then incinerate them. We did not live in a time of asylums or places that can care for people, so they would rid the world of them by simply calling them something that they weren't, then killing them off."

"But tonight, they're planning this big party to kill off a few people that are in their way." Lelani and Caroline both nodded at Keion. "Christ, this is worse than I thought it was going to be. They've taken something so horrific and turned it in to something they can profit from. How can we keep this from happening again down the road?"

"We can't." Keion thought that Lelani was kidding, but he realized that she was telling him a fact. "All we can do is slow them down a bit before it gets well out of control. People can and will murder for any kind of reason. How they do it, how they bring their own form of justice to someone, is never something you can count on. What you can count on, however, is that people will take something and twist it up into something so totally different than what it started out as and make it work for them. There were bad witches, there still are. And it might have started out with the Herald killing them off when they got out of control. But then people got it in their head that they could use it for their own sort of gain. Get rid of a mother-in-law that is living with an already too large family. A neighbor that is encroaching on their land at times by letting his sheep eat the grass they own. Even someone that has nothing more to do with them than they might have slighted them unknowingly. It's one of the main reasons that I have stayed alone, kept away from people for so long."

He could certainly understand that now. As the rest of them talked about the meeting tonight and the plans that they were making, he thought of the things he'd seen over his lifetime. And he realized that Lelani was right. People sucked. Well, not all of them, but the few who did sure made it terrible for the rest of the world.

They were going to meet at the field an hour before the men were to gather. The wives, girlfriends, and a few others that had been invited were coming an hour after the meeting started, they'd been told. Keion thought it was like bringing a last meal to those men who were to be killed. Or a better one would have been bringing lambs to the slaughter. As they prepared for the meeting, Lelani went to talk to the dragons with the help of Lindsey. He asked to talk to Asher.

"These men, do you know what we're going to say to them? How we're going to take care that they stop?" Asher said that they'd try to talk, but he doubted that it would work. "I'm worried that they'll hurt Lelani. She's pretty powerful, and they'll go after her first of all."

"They'll try." Keion said he didn't think that was a good thing. "No, not for them anyway. They're going to come up.... Let me ask you something, Keion. Are you worried for her or for the men that are going to wish to Christ that they'd never heard of the Herald and the men who run that group? Because they're not going to know what the fuck hit them when they try anything. Lelani alone can take them, of that I have no doubt. But with all of us there? And the dragons too? They are going to be so terrified that they'll not even think about hurting her."

He hoped so. But in his experience, and he'd been around as long as Asher, nothing was ever as easy or as simple as it looked. There was always that one fucking idiot that would do something so out of character for himself that people would die. Keion decided that whether or not it was part of the plan, he was going to be his dragon so he could get in, do some serious damage, then get her out. He told Shane his plan.

"I agree with you. We'll stand beside her, but you are better equipped to keep her safe than I am." He was so glad that Shane agreed with him that he let out the breath he'd been holding. He just knew he was going to tell him that she'd be fine too. "But you have to promise me that you're going to be safe as well. I can't stand the thought of anything happening to either of you."

"I swear to you that I won't try to get hurt." Shane told him that wasn't what he meant. "I know it's not, but I'm not

149

going to stand back and let any of us get hurt if I can help it. And if it means I get hurt, then so be it. Hurt can heal. Dead? There is no coming back from that."

As they worked on the castle—very little had to be done right now as it was still moving into place—Keion wondered if other dragons were on their way. So far, at last count, there were over sixty of them. Then there were the brownies and faeries that seemed to come in daily. Just last week he'd been flying overhead on his way to the quarry when he saw a group of larger dragons playing in the fields. It was a sight that he thought not long ago that he'd ever see. And now, just because of his mom and dad making it possible, they were finding out that they weren't the last of their kind. It was the most amazing thing.

Chapter 8

Everything was in place. Robert had had to call in a few favors, a lot of them actually, to have food brought in. And a few promises that he'd not been sure of at first, but was warming to the idea of killing someone off for the services he wanted. Right now he had three women, all of them chained up in the sublevels of the charter house they were using, ready to be slaughtered. His dick got hard just thinking about the three of them chained to the walls and naked. He wanted to go down there and take the one with the big tits again.

He'd gone down to check on them after the six men who had brought them in took them to the basement and tied them up. When it seemed to him that they were taking a very long time to do something so simple, he'd gone down to check on them. They were fucking the women while they were chained up, and Robert had nearly come in his pants when he watched one of the men slap the woman he'd been fucking.

Robert had never thought of himself as a sadist. But fuck, it was hot watching those women being held there, their arms and legs bolted to the walls and their pussies right where a man could fuck them. The men hadn't even bothered to strip down, just pulled down their pants far enough to free their dicks and slam them into them.

"You want a try?" He looked at the man who was fisting his cock while he seemed to be waiting his turn. "I never done it like this before, but when those two did it first, I thought what the fuck. Ain't even my wife that I'm fucking, either."

He watched the men, three of them with their pants down around their asses, taking the women hard and fast. When one of them stumbled back, the man he'd been talking to moved in and starting fucking the woman. Robert moved closer, just close enough, he told himself, to make sure that they weren't hurting them. But as soon as he saw the dick of the man closest to him going in and out of the woman, Robert felt his own dick fill up and hurt with need. Then he saw her.

The woman had the biggest tits he'd ever seen. Not only were they as big as cantaloupes, but her nipples looked to be about two inches long and as thick as his thumb and more. His mouth watered to suckle one of them into his mouth. Hell, he wanted to fuck them. When it was his turn with her, he pulled his pants down fast enough that he nearly took his dick off.

But instead of fucking her, he took her breast into his mouth and did just what he wanted, suckled at her. And when a ripe sweet taste filled his mouth, he looked up at her.

"Ever since I had me boobs, I've had me milk in them. You go on now and fill your belly with it. Mother's milk is good for your cock." He nodded and suckled at her again. "That's it baby, momma is gonna feed her baby. You give me that cock of yours and we'll see if we can have us a little fun."

He wanted to take her down, to lay her out over the table and take her hard while she squirted her milk over him. When he slammed his cock into her, she cried out and he lifted her breast up for him to suck. But before he could do that, milk sprayed him in the face and on his chest.

It was by far the most erotic thing he'd ever had done to him. Fucking her harder, her breast in his mouth again, he used his other hand to milk her. Christ, his body was soaked with her milk. And when he came, throwing back his head and fucking her deeper, she cried out as well and sprayed him all over his chest and face with both breasts.

Staggering away from her, his dick still semi hard, he watched as another man took her. Robert wanted to shove him out of the way and fuck her again and again. But before he could have another go at her, he was called away. Christ, he hated being in charge at times.

"Are you listening to me?" Robert looked at the man standing beside him and nodded. "You have not been listening to me. You look like you've been.... What the fuck is on you? You're all sticky, like you've bathed in ice cream or something."

"Or something." He adjusted his cock. "What is it you brought me up here for? I'm assuming that everything is going as we planned."

"Sort of. The stake isn't working out the way we wanted it to. According to your notes, it's supposed to be four feet in the ground with five cords of wood around it. Your ancestors, that's the way they said it had to be, and were very specific about the rules for burning a witch and making sure that her magic didn't harm those around them. But when we load it up that way, there isn't any room for the witch."

It was the most ridiculous thing he'd ever seen when he looked at it now. It looked like there was maybe a foot at the top of the stake, and there was so much wood around it that he was hard pressed to not laugh. He turned to Wilbur, the man who had been helping him prepare for this thing, and had to let out a long breath or two before he could speak.

"How tall did it say the stake had to be?" Wilbur scratched his head and said he'd not checked on that. "And I'm pretty sure that when it said five cords of wood, it meant that you put them there after the witch was on the stake. It might have been roomier for you had you done it that way."

"Yeah, I can see where that might be helpful. I was really wondering how I was going to get my wife up there on that little bitty thing. She's a larger woman." Robert was still a bit squeamish about this whole thing. "I'll get to that right now."

He had fools working with him. And the worst part was, Wilbur was probably the smartest one in the whole group. Every time he had a chance to look around, the men were talking about what it was going to be like to be without their loved one. He wondered if a single one of them had given any thought to what it was going to be like to burn someone alive. His own plans were to simply kill his wife by breaking her fucking neck. He'd even watched videos on how to hold her to make it a clean break. Christ, he wondered what else he might find on the Internet, and decided to find out when this shit was done. But there wasn't any way he was hanging around when the women were burned. Fucking some nice tits was what he was planning.

He'd been out cooking burgers for his wife and son yesterday when it hit him it would be like this. The sizzling sound, the way the meat burned up. He had to go to the bushes and throw up twice before he was able to take them off the grill and into the house. And Robert had not been able to eat a single bite of them. It was just too much. Yet here he was going along with this like he had not a single care in the world.

As he made his way to the building—he told himself it was to check on things—he felt the air get warmer around him. Turning to see if the fools had set the fire already, he fell back on his ass when a dragon—a real live, mother fucking giant dragon—landed on the ground in front of him. Two men—he didn't even know their names—were crushed beneath the beast's foot. And when the dragon turned and set fire to the stakes that had been set up, Robert watched them burn in abject horror.

"Hello, Robert. I told you I'd be back." He looked at the woman in front of him, tearing his eyes away from the single stake that had not been scorched. Like it was there just for him. The others, the ones with all the wood stacked up around them, were burning out of control. "What the fuck do you think you're doing here?"

"Dragon. He's.... There's fire.... There's a dragon on the.... Did you see that?" She turned and looked, then looked back at him. "There is a dragon there."

155

"Yes, I'm well aware of it. I rode in here on him. And I brought more. Would you like to see them as well?" He nodded, then shook his head. His entire body was hot now, the chill in the day completely gone now that the dragon had shown up. But before he could ask Lelani if she really had ridden in here on the back of a dragon, six more dragons, smaller but no less dangerous, landed near her. "This is my family, and you've fucked with the wrong group."

"Family? You're a witch *and* a dragon?" He started to stand but a long blade, like ones he'd seen in medieval movies, was put at his throat. Robert looked up at the man standing over him. It was as if he were in a surreal movie and he'd not gotten a script. "You're wearing a crown."

His mind, he thought, had simply shut off. A man in a pair of blue jeans, a sweatshirt, and a crown was holding a sword at his throat that looked to have more jewels on it than he'd seen in any shop. The crown was just as covered and beautiful. The need to touch the blade, even to see if it was as sharp as it looked, had him lifting his hand up.

"You touch that and he'll be obligated to remove your empty head." Robert snatched his hand back so quickly that he felt the bite of the blade cut into him. "Now, this is how this conversation is going to go. You're going to disband this merry group of men, give me the book that you have been using, and free the women you have in the basement."

"I didn't fuck them." He snapped his mouth closed when he realized what he'd said. The man and Lelani laughed. "What I meant to say was, I didn't bring them here."

"But you did intend to burn them, didn't you? By the way, I'd like you to meet my brother-in-law, Asher, king of the dragons. You can't lie to him. So when he asks you a question, you'll tell him the truth. The reason that I'm making sure you understand that is because there is someone else here I'd like for you to meet. But then, I'm pretty sure you know him as well. Agent Dominic Fitzpatrick. He's the man in charge of investigating the death of Beth Herald and Peter Winebarger. You remember them, don't you?"

"I want you to stop this right now." She laughed again. "I swear to you, on my son's heart, that I will cease this right now and you'll never be bothered by me and my group again. You can even have my book. It's in the basement in the safe. But you have to send him away and leave me in peace. I've decided that this is not what I set out for." He gave her the combination and she turned and nodded to another man, who left them.

Asher, the huge king, pulled out a sheet of paper. It was almost comical to see him dressed as he was when the man next to him was in a suit and tie. When a dragon about the size of a tall man came to stand next to Lelani, he wondered if he was going to get a break and the dragon would eat her. Instead of something going his way, the dragon put his great head on her shoulder and purred.

"This is my husband, Keion. My other husband is coming now with your book. I told you before that you were messing with the wrong family here. And I'm going to be thrilled to death to know that I, a mere woman and witch, was able to bring you down."

It occurred to him then, something that Cybil had told him not long ago. "You're the daughter. The daughter of

Mary Wayne and one of my relatives. Your mother really was a witch? And you have a fucking dragon as a mate? Christ, my family will never believe this." She told him no one would. "What do you mean? You're right there. And Fitzpatrick there, he can see them."

"See what? The only thing I've seen, Herald, is a man that is about to confess to a lot of crimes on my books. Now then, Asher, if you'd be so—"

"Wait a minute. You have to see them. There are...." He looked around the people and counted. "There are eight dragons here. Eight of them. And one of them is as big as a house. You cannot expect me to believe that you can't see them. They're right fucking there."

Instead of looking around, the man only cleared his throat. This was ridiculous, Robert thought, there wasn't any way that they couldn't see them. Christ, the one that Lelani had claimed to have ridden upon was laying down with his eyes closed. Like it was fucking boring to him to be here.

"Robert James Herald, did you kill Bethany Winebarger Herald?" He tried to keep his tongue between his teeth by biting it. But it did no good when Asher asked him again. "Did you kill Peter Winebarger, father to Bethany, your wife?"

"Yes. Fuck yes. They were going to throw me out of my own home." Asher asked him if Beth had asked him for a divorce. "No, she flat out told me that she was filing. I thought for sure that she had, but nothing ever came of it."

"And Lynne Hardgrave Herald, were you planning to kill her as well?" Robert told him that he was. It really was as if he couldn't lie to him. "What of your son? Was he on your list as well?"

"My son? No, why would he have to die? He is my heir. And someone who is going to carry on the Herald works. Did you know that my father never did a thing about this?" He laughed, feeling his head spin around at what he was seeing with his own eyes. "If he was here now, do you have any idea what he'd think? Hell, I'd bet you a buck that he'd piss his pants."

"Did you kill Erin, my sister?" Robert looked at Lelani and nodded, and felt his mind simply snap when he watched the great dragon lick her neck. He wondered again if he was going to eat her, but knew that he couldn't be so lucky. "I should just let him kill you."

"The cop, the king, or the dragon?" Robert let the burble of laughter escape from his mouth. "Sounds like a nursery rhyme, doesn't it? The cop, the king, and the dragon went to town. The townspeople were so afraid. Do you think he might eat us asked the townspeople? I don't know, said the man, we'll have to wait and see."

He was still going on about his town and the dragon when he was shoved toward a car. Robert knew that he was going to prison, for a great many years. But he'd tell his story, let everyone he knew know about the dragons and witches he'd seen this day.

"Robert?" He turned and looked at the woman standing next to him. She was gorgeous, and it took him several seconds to realize it was his wife, Lynne. She had gotten dressed up, her hair done. When he asked her how she had afforded that, she smiled at him and he thought of the dragon with the sharp horn on his head. The way his tale had swung around, taking down the burning stakes. "You're not going to say a word about the dragons and witches here today. Do you want to know why?"

He just laughed and asked her to take a selfie with him and one of the larger ones. "That way when they tell me I'm insane, which I might just be, I'll have this picture. Come on now, you know you want to be famous as well."

"Not really." When she drew a knife and swiped it through the air, he felt strangely detached for a moment. Then warmth slowly saturated his chest, and his shirt felt damp. When he looked down, blood was flowing from his neck and he wanted to reach up to stop it. But he was unable to as his hands were tied behind his back. "You're going to rot in hell, Robert. Last of the Heralds. My son, the little one that you cherished so much? He's not yours. I thought you'd like to tell that to your long dead grand-whatever when you see him in hell."

Robert felt himself fall to his knees. There would be no saving him, he knew this. Nor would they care to. He knew as surely as he was falling to the ground that he'd been a horrific person. But to be honest, he wasn't sure if he might have been much different had he been given the chance. His life, he thought with a smile, had been fucking fantastic. And he'd been able to see a real dragon. Wait until he told someone about that.

~~~

"We have eleven in custody and two more that we're trying to gather up. When the dragons landed, they scattered like dust bunnies." Shane nodded, his attention on Lelani and the woman that had been arrested for the murder of Robert.

But Allen Lance, a friend and a wolf that worked at the police station, seemed to understand. "She more than likely won't survive the trial. I just found out that she has cancer."

"And her son? What will happen to him?" Allen said that there was a grandmother, and they were trying to contact her now. "Let me know what you find out. If she can't or doesn't want him, I'll talk to my wife. Perhaps we can arrange something."

Allen nodded and looked where Shane was looking. "She's strong. I know you more than likely know that, but what she did here today, that's more than I've ever thought of having a witch do."

"She said that she didn't want anyone hurt but those that deserved it. When Silco landed on those two men, I thought for sure that she was going to be upset. But they killed their wives this morning in anticipation of seeing them burn at the stake." Shane looked at his longtime friend. "Doesn't love mean anything to humans anymore?"

"I can't answer that, Shane. I surely can't. Two months ago I came upon a house that had four little ones in it and not a bit of food. The eldest told me that it had been a week since he'd had anything in his belly as his momma had her welfare cut off." Shane asked if she tried to get it returned to her. "Can't. She and her kids are suffering in ways you cannot believe. The husband took what little money there was. The electric had been shut off, and they were in dire need of transportation. I helped her out a little, but that's taking from my own kids' mouths too."

"Send her around to the antique store tomorrow. I'll make

161

sure that Jed is aware of her situation and what they need." Allen thanked him. "And I'm serious about that little boy of Robert's. There is no reason for him to be put in the system if we can help it."

When all the men there were arrested, and the women freed that had been brought in, the police were going to do a door to door search of the homes. No one was sure what they would find, but nothing so far had been ordinary, so they didn't expect this to be either. Shane gathered Lelani in his arms when they were told they could go.

"She said that he'd made arrangements before he left this morning for her to come out here tonight. Robert told her that they were going to have a nice dinner and then stay at a hotel. Lynne found out today that he'd lost his job and there wasn't enough money to buy food for them. And the mortgage was behind for the last four months." Shane held her tighter in his arms as she continued. "Lynne said she only came out here to confront him about the job and to ask him what they were going to do. Then she heard him say he had plans to kill her. I guess that was what took her over the edge."

"Allen said that she didn't come armed, so that'll work in her favor. He also said that she never mentioned the dragons. Did you do that?" She turned in his arms then and laid her head on his chest. Keion was taking care of the building with Silco so that no one would come out here again thinking to take up where the men had left off. "Lelani, I have a favor to ask of you. And Keion, but you first. There is a chance that Robert's little boy will be put in the system after today."

"We'll take him. We'll end the violence in his family by raising him up to be a good solid man." She looked up at him.

"Is that the favor? To bring him to our home?"

"Yes. But I've been thinking we should spread around some of our wealth. The three of us, we have more than enough, and should we need more, there is our portion of the things that were put aside for our families to use. I want to help some families out that might otherwise go to bed hungry tonight." She told him she'd do whatever he wanted. "Good. I'd like to start by opening up a business. I'm not sure what it would be, but something that we can hire a few people and get them trained. Allen said there is a woman whose husband left her with their children without means of support, and they're hungry."

She pulled away from him and moved to the car. When she stopped and looked at him, he asked her what she was doing. Lelani grinned at him and opened the door to her truck that his dad had brought over for them.

"We have to buy food. And find some shelter for them too. Do you know if they have coats for winter? I would bet not. And furniture too. Do you suppose that there is anything open this...? What are you doing now?" He just shook his head and moved to the passenger side of her truck. Roger leapt in the back end and laid down. He'd have to be dropped off at the house, but his dad decided to come along.

"I've been thinking that we need to get us a few things in town too. Did you know that there are televisions as big as me? Durn near had me a fit when Simeon told me about it. And then he pulled one up on his phone for me to see. I could use one of them." Shane asked his dad what he'd watch on it. "Never you mind about that. I can find me something to look at on it. And I'm gonna be watching me some things with them girls of mine too. Never too old to start watching things with them. And with Christmas coming up in only four months, I'm thinking I need to get me a start on things there too."

"You can order them online and have them delivered to your house, too." Shane was glad he was looking at his dad when Lelani said that to him, or he might not have had the best laugh he'd had in a month. "Not to mention, you can even have someone come out and put whatever it is you buy together."

"I suppose the next thing you'll be telling me is that they'll even wrap it all up with a pretty bow too." When Lelani nodded, it was all Shane could do not to have her pull over so he could stand up. Sitting down and laughing this hard hurt. "Now I done heard it all. Yes, sir, I heard about it all."

Chapter 9

Lelani wasn't sure what to do with a kid. She'd been one so long ago that it was just a blur for her. Even being around the babies, who wouldn't know to judge her just yet if she messed up, was enough to send her to the outdoors. What was she going to do with a seven-year-old little boy in the house?

His mother was dead. No one had told him as yet, but she'd committed suicide in her hospital room late yesterday afternoon. The note that she'd left had told whoever read it that she was finished with life; there didn't seem to be much reason to live out the last of her days in a prison cell. Then she wished her son well. Then at the end she explained how she had lied to Robert about his son, and wished now that she'd not been so cruel.

The house was empty but for the four of them. Roger was in the kitchen preparing lunch and the three of them were pacing the front hall. She supposed that it was her pacing, and Shane and Keion were moving out of her way.

"I'm glad that you asked the rest of your family to give us some time to talk to him first." Shane said if it was overwhelming for her, he had no idea what it would be for a kid. "No kidding. You're all so big too. If I were short, I'd run screaming when you guys were around."

They expected him in an hour. Sooner if traffic would cooperate. It was too soon for her, and not soon enough for Mark Herald to arrive. The kid had had a hell of a two weeks since his mom had killed his dad. And even though he didn't know it, he'd also been rejected by a grandmother, and his mom had left him alone in the world.

The car pulled up ten minutes early. Her heart had been beating pretty fast up until then, but now it felt as if it were going to bounce its way right out of her chest. Keion came to stand on her other side and Shane went to open the door. This was it, he was coming to live with them.

For the week after he was taken into foster care, her and Shane or Keion would go and visit him every day. She wasn't sure what to think at first. Mark's grandma had told them that her daughter was a murderer and she didn't want a thing to do with a murderer's son. Fucking bitch. Lelani didn't want to get too attached to him—though at first visit she fell in love with the little guy—in the event that he wasn't going to be staying with them. Had Lelani had her way, the grandma would have joined her son-in-law and daughter in the morgue.

166

Going out on the deck when the car came to a stop, she waited for the door to open before she moved down to the driveway. With each step she took closer to the car, the more terrified she became. What the hell were they thinking?

You got this. Lelani looked around for the source of the voice that seemed to float over the wind, and saw no one. The words, she'd heard them before, and it took her a moment to remember where. Taking a stumbling step and only just catching herself, she remembered who had said that to her time and time again.

"Hello." Shaking off the memories, she went down on her knees to be eye level with Mark. He still looked sad, his little face thinner than it had been before. "They said that if you didn't like me or want me, I could go back to the big house."

"Do you want to go back there?" He looked at Mrs. Peirce, then at her. "You can if you want. But if you decide to stay, then that's a done deal. We're all ready for you to come and be with us, but if you've changed your mind, now would be the time to do it."

"I'm afraid." Lelani told him she understood that, she was too. "But you're a big person. Not a kid like me. I don't want you to hate me too."

"Are you talking about your grandmother?" He nodded and wiped at the tears, and told her he was sorry. "Don't be sorry. You need to cry, then go for it. Once, when I was about your age, a woman told me that you cry to wash out the bad things. If you just keep them in, like bad thoughts, then they'll fester and boil over into the good things in your life. Do you want that to happen?"

"No. But what if you think that, 'cause my mom killed my dad, I might be too much for you too?" She told him it wasn't going to happen. "Mom, she said that Dad had been a bad man. I don't understand that. He wasn't always nice to Mom, but he was okay with me. He never took me places like he said he would, but he was really busy supporting us."

They had already decided not to bad mouth either his mom or his dad. Someday, when he was ready and wanted to know, they'd tell him what had happened. Keion had started saving the newspapers too, in the event he wanted to know what they had to say about his parents someday.

"Shane has gotten you a fishing pole, and your new grandda will take you fishing whenever you want to go when it's warmer. You have two cousins already here, and more on the way too sometime, I bet." He looked over at Jacob when she did. "He is so excited to have you hanging out with him. Jacob is a good man and will never hurt you."

Mark turned back to her, his face almost as readable as an open book. He was both terrified and excited. While he wanted to believe that they'd never turn him out, there were other things as well, things that she'd told him that he had to deal with when he was alone.

She wanted him to know about all of the things he might see here. And there were plenty. But she also told him that it had to be a secret, because there were people living with them that needed to feel safe around him. Safe so that bad people didn't come and hurt them too. She took one of the brownies with her once, just to prove to him what sort of magical things his secrets were keeping safe.

"You remember what I told you? About the dragons and

faeries?" He looked at Mrs. Peirce again when she patted him on the back and left without saying a word. "I sent her on her way. I'm thinking you're ready to stay."

"Yes. I am. You said I could meet a faerie. But I had to keep it a secret." She nodded and put out her hand. When a little brownie landed in her hand, Mark took a small step back. But he never took his eyes off the little man. "What's his name?"

"I'm Peck. This is my lovely mate. She'll be helping in the household." Peck and his mate bowed low and stood up. "You'd be Master Mark, correct? If you want, and I have permission from the king of dragons and the faerie queen, I can be your friend. We can anyway, but this way, we can live together the rest of our days." As they stood there, talking, the little woman faerie flew off to the house.

"You mean that you'd live with me in the house? That would be really cool. Do you think we can hang out together all the time?" Peck said he had no reason to think that they couldn't. "I don't have much. The house where I was living with the foster care, they said that I'd have to give up my things. I didn't have much anyways. We were kinda poor."

As the two of them moved into the house, Lelani stood up and watched them. Peck knew the lay of the house and which room was going to be Mark's, so she had no doubt that was where they were headed now. As the door shut behind them, she could hear Mark telling Peck what had been going on *his entire life*. All seven years of it.

"I think we've just been out done by a speck." She told Shane his name was Peck. "Same thing. We're not as cool anymore."

"I don't think we were ever cool." They all three laughed as they made their way into the house. Jacob joined them when Roger was just handing them tall glasses of tea. "Dad, you should have seen him. Every emotion you could imagine running over his face until Peck showed up."

"He mention fishing? I been scouting out the best places for him and me to go." Lelani told Jacob that Mark didn't care for fishing. The look on his face was so heartbreaking that she told him she was teasing. "Not nice. And here I thought you and me was going to be the best of buds now. You shouldn't scare an old man like that. Dern near sent me on a twizzle swizzle."

She wasn't sure what that meant, but she would never tease him like that again. And later, after Mark and Peck had looked over the entire house, they joined them in the kitchen. All in all, she thought it went very well. But when dinner time rolled around, Peck came to find her.

"I think the young master is afraid of the dark, miss." She started to stand up to go to him when Keion said he'd go. "Very good, sir. He's not wanting to be upset in front of the missus, if you know what I mean."

When Keion returned half an hour later with Mark in tow, all he said was that things were fine now. She was sure they were, but after dinner decided to go by his room when she went up later that night. Opening the door quietly, she was surprised to find two of the smaller dragons in the room with him, as well as one of the faeries. Blue, the faerie, said she was there to keep the dragons from harm. The dragons were sitting in the windows, one on each side of the bed.

"We've come to ward off the bad men." She asked them what bad men. "Don't know, my lady. But Keion said that the young master was fearful of them, and we should keep an eye out for them. I'm thinking it might have been about his father."

Carefully so as not to wake Mark, she touched her fingers to his head to see who might have scared him. When she sat on the edge of the bed after finding the information, she turned to the dragons.

"His father would sometimes fight with his mom late at night, and he'd tell her about what his family did to the witches of their time. I'm hoping they thought him asleep and never dreamed that he was hearing every horrid detail." Peck came to sit on the pillow by Mark's head as she continued. "He's afraid that some of the men who would gather witches would come and find him and burn him at the stake by mistake."

"Oh, the poor lad. To think that someone could be so careless with their words." Lelani agreed. "Mistress, are you going to remove those memories from him? He might sleep better if you were to do that."

She had actually thought about it, to save him from suffering needlessly. But it wouldn't be right. On a great many levels.

"No. I can't do that. If I do, it's messing with the timeline of his life. While I know very little about his future, I can tell you that his memories that he makes now, here with us, are going to soon push the bad ones away about his father and mother." Peck thought that a good thing then. "Yes. I have to agree. Whatever is there, it will mold him into the man that

171

he'll become. A great man."

As she left the room, she thanked the tiny dragons for their help, and both said it was their pleasure to help the tiny human. She wondered if either of them realized that he outweighed them by thirty pounds or more, and he was only going to get bigger. As she left the room in favor of her own, she was smiling. Things might just be all right.

~~~

The castle was, but for a few things, finished. They still needed to cut the trees for the front gate and to fill it with the things that had been stored away. Shane put his hand on the wall that was closest to the fireplace and felt the warmth of it. It was warm, not just from the fire that now blazed in the large open fireplace, but there was love there. He could feel it in every part of the place now.

"Do you suppose we should start bringing up the bigger pieces in the morning?" He looked at Asher when he asked and realized that his brother was king of this place. "What?"

"We're not going to have to call you anything like kingie, are we? And I hope to Christ you don't think you're going to rule from a big chair, either." Asher flushed a deep red. "You were thinking that, weren't you?"

"No. No, it's not that, but.... Well, come with me. And before you make any kind of comment on this, know that Dad got them for Essie and me. I'm taking away his Internet access too, as of now." As they entered the large room that they'd figured out was the throne room, Shane had to put his hand over his mouth and hold the laughter ready to spill out. He looked at his dad as he made his way to them, and could see that he was quite proud of himself.

"They were just gonna burn it in the wood pile." Shane wanted to ask why someone didn't let them. "But I gave the man ten dollars and asked him to bring them out here. Don't you think they're something?"

"They're something, all right." The chairs—he supposed one could call them that—were matching and had a place to sit your bottom. But other than that, their relationship with a "chair" ended there. "You only paid ten dollars for these?"

As his dad went on about how he'd gotten such a wonderful deal on them, he walked closer. They did not improve on closer inspection. In actuality, he was hard pressed to understand why someone would have built them in the first place.

The arms of them were made of what looked to him like moose antlers. Big ones too, that would fit a small child in them if they wanted to sit there. The points of the antlers stood over the seat of the chair about two feet, and they were polished to a high gleam that hurt the eyes when the sun flickered over them. When he touched his fingers to it, he realized at once they were made of plastic and not from a real moose. Christ.

The back of the seat was covered in fake zebra fur. He knew it was fake because the stripes were perfectly lined up with one another, and even went so far as to look like someone had taken a marker to them to straighten out a few places where the fur had worn thin. Running his hand over the material, he thought he'd never sit in these suckers; the fur felt like a thousand pins sticking straight up. And upon inspecting his fingers, he realized that if someone did sit in them, they'd be covered in tiny little black and white spikes of the *fur* all the time.

As he moved to the front of them again, he looked at the legs and had to hide his reaction when he realized what they were. They were fashioned into rhino feet, four of them, with hooves and all. Shane thought he might hurt tomorrow from holding in his laughter every time he thought of Essie and Asher sitting up here.

He was still laughing when Lelani entered the room. She took one look at the pair of chairs and stopped dead in her tracks. "Oh dear Lord. What the hell are those? Did someone actually save those for you guys?"

"No, I bought them for this room." Lelani just stared at Dad then back at the chairs. "What do you think of them?"

"Think? I think they're the ugliest things I ever saw. I mean, Christ almighty, I can't believe someone didn't hit you when you went to pick them up. Please tell me that you didn't pay anything for them. Hell, I'm not sure why you weren't paid to take them away. Those are horrid." Shane started toward her when it was obvious to him that she was going to continue to talk badly about his dad's purchase. "Jacob, I think you need to get out more if you think this is high fashion."

His dad started dancing around the room and laughing then. "I knew it. I just knew it. I told Elbert it would be you that told me I was off my noodle. You were a mite nicer about it than I thought you'd be, however. But he owes me ten dollars." Asher asked him if it had been a joke all along. "Well of course it was. You don't think I have that poor of taste, do you? My goodness, son, I'm not addled."

Shane couldn't help it, he laughed so hard and for so long that he had to lay on the hard floor to breathe. And he might have been all right sooner, but every time he looked at the chairs, he laughed again. Christ, they really were the ugliest things he'd ever seen.

His dad looked so sad for a moment, and he was sure that they'd hurt his feelings despite the fact that he'd told them it was a joke. Sitting up, he asked his dad if he was all right. With a short nod, he started talking.

"When the king was in this room that night, there were curtains made of the purest silk that hung in long streams that touched the floor. I was nervous, you know, but I did have a chance to have me a look-see. They weren't too practical, but they sure were pretty. The other room, the only other one I'd been in back then, had tapestries on each wall as big as a man. It was said that they were brought to the castle so long before King Anthony came there that it was surprising that they'd not been sold off or destroyed." His dad looked around the room, and Shane thought of the only other time he'd been here. The night that he'd met his wife, mother to Shane and the rest of them. "Sally and I were thrown together that night. The king sat me right down on his lady wife's chair and spoke to me like he'd known me all my life. I guess he did in a way, since he was one to come and visit a person when they needed it. He was a good man. A better leader than we'd ever seen before."

"The night that he was killed, you said you could hear the doors being pushed against. Do you remember how long after you were taken away that you knew that he had fallen?" Asher sat on the big chair, then got up and sat on the floor. It was funny really, but Shane didn't say anything. Before his

175

dad could answer Asher, the rest of them, all of them, joined them in the room. They brought in lawn chairs and food to munch on. The table, the massive one that had been made for this room, was the only other piece of furniture besides the chairs.

The furniture that had been built by the specifications in the book had been delivered just yesterday. And some of the bigger pieces, like this one, had to be assembled in the castle. The only way that those pieces would ever leave here would be either to burn them or to take them apart again. And they were heavy too. Running his hand over the smooth glossy surface of the table, he listened to his father tell the story he'd heard a thousand times over the years.

"He was nearly gone by the time I was brought to him. He'd been stabbed several times as he tried to save his queen. Elbert said that the king was hurt and that there wasn't much time when he came to my home to get me. When I was near enough to him to touch, I saw the pool of blood in his lap and under his chair. He held on, I'm sure, to talk to me and my Sally. At first, when I heard the big doors shake, I thought for sure that he'd brought me there to stand beside him when the men came in. And they were coming in too. The walls to the keep had been breached already. It was only a matter of time before they were in this chamber with us." Dad walked to the dais and sat on the highest step. "He knew; I know that now. Knew beforehand that he'd die, that Queen Eve would as well. I oftentimes wonder what might have been going through their heads then. How they would have coped with knowing that they'd never see some of the things that they'd put here come to fruition. Their children would have been killed had anyone known about them, so they had taken steps to assure that no one knew of them. Even the fact that the queen had given birth to six hatchlings would have been something that the fanatics — yes, we had them even then — would have launched on quick enough. Then there is the fact that they moved all the things from their home to the lower levels, a little at a time and without anyone knowing what they were about, to save it for you. Can you imagine the kind of other things that were going on in their heads? I can't. Not even a little. I would have only been thinking of my children and not being able to see them grow into men."

"The vision that they had only showed them that the castle had fallen. Not that they would perish, nor did they know what was to become of their children." Caroline took up the story from Dad. "Then the morning after she'd given birth, as she lay there with them, she saw it all, she told me. The women in their lives, the children that they would have. She cried that day and well into the next, telling me bits and pieces of what she had learned."

"She knew they were to die then?" Caroline nodded at Keion. "Wasn't there anything they could have done? Could one of them been saved to have been here with us?"

"Oh no. Not with those two. Their love was a match for all time. While they knew that they'd miss their children and seeing them grow up, they knew that they could ensure that they'd be all right and live through the people that they set in your paths. But they would never leave this earth without the other. Anthony told me once, long ago, that he only breathed because of his Eve. That his heart only beat because hers did.

He was a romantic too." Shane pulled Lelani closer to him, and Keion moved closer to them as well. "Every spring he'd take her to the top of the mountain and they'd watch the blossoms open on the cherry tree there. I was so pleased when one was planted to replace it."

"The mountain asked for it."

Caroline nodded, as if she had figured that out. And when they were ready to move through the castle, they did so as a group, taking each floor, each room, as a family. A family that was bound together by the people who had made this all possible.

Chapter 10

Gracie Hobbs unloaded her backpack and pulled out her sleeping bag. It was colder in the mountains than she'd thought it would be, but it was still wonderful to be here. As she lay on the bag, she looked up at the cloudless sky and thought of her journey so far. And it had been one.

It had taken a great deal of nerve for her to start out, but now that she was a month into her adventure, she was so glad that she'd done it. Backpacking across the United States had given her the perfect way to relax, and to remove herself from life for a little while.

Her mother was going through a time. Gracie wasn't really sure what she meant when she told her and her sister that. Just that she was selling the house that they'd grown up in and moving. She had no destination in mind, nor how she was going to get there if she did. Nor did she know what she was going to do for a place to live when she returned. She was just doing it.

"I think Mom is off her rocker." Gracie asked her sister, Cora, why she thought that. Not that she didn't think the same thing, but maybe she had a solid reason for thinking that. "Did you know that she's cashed in all Dad's stocks, and means to empty her accounts too?"

"Well, it's sort of her money. Her house too, really. It's not like either of us lived there anymore. And she did give us what we wanted out of it." Cora just rolled her eyes. Gracie had noted to herself just the week before how Cora did that a great deal when she didn't like her answers. "Mom always lands on her feet. I'm sure this won't be any different."

"Well, I'm not going to be taking her in if she comes back broke and dumber." Gracie said nothing. "And if you think to bully me into it, I'll be really pissed at you."

"Okay, first? I have never in my life bullied you into anything. You have always done as you pleased regardless of how it might affect others." Cora lifted her chin as if to say, so what. "Secondly, as I said, Mom will be fine. If she wants to run off to some country or join a cult, I'm sure that she'll have more fun than you do at your stupid country club meetings and mommy groups."

Cora had laughed. "You're jealous. Oh my God, how did I not see this before? You're jealous because I have a wonderful life, a great husband and children, and money to burn. You hate me for that." Gracie said she didn't hate anyone. "Of course not. You go right on thinking that. And in the meantime, I want you to think about your own life and how it's so messed up."

Two weeks after their mom left for Rome and other countries, Gracie stored her few belongings in a storage locker, bought a book on backpacking, and left. She had a nice hefty savings account and all her bills were caught up. She was going to use her money to have some "me" time. Cora had called her two days later, when Gracie had decided that she'd had enough of walking and hurting.

"You fool." Gracie sat up on her sleeping bag and had asked Cora what she meant. "You're just doing this to piss me off. Come home and forget this foolishness. I swear to Christ, am I the only sane one in this family? Get home and we'll discuss how stupid you've been to just quit your job and sell your things. And then I want you to check yourself into one of those health spas. Not the one I go to, but one that is cheaper for you."

"Why on earth would I do any of that? Just because you told me to?" Her sister said it was better than what she was doing now. "I see. Better for you or for me?"

"Do you have any idea what my friends are saying right now? I can't control my mother. I can't control you. I don't have time to keep bailing you out of every little scrap you get into." Gracie asked her what scraps she was talking about. "Well this, for one thing. You've quit your job and moved out of your home. I suppose you're going to expect me to bail you out of this, aren't you?"

"I'm on vacation right now, my rent is paid up, and no, I'm not expecting any more out of you now than I usually get. You've not been very involved in my life for longer than I can remember, so this shouldn't surprise you when I say, back off. I don't need to be bailed out. I'm a grown woman who can make up her own mind without you harping on me all the time." Cora told her to act like it and get back to reality. "Believe it or not, until you called, I was ready to do just that. But thankfully you called and made me change my mind."

"You mean you're coming home. Good. I don't want to have to call the police and have them bring you back. You're being completely immature, and I think you're being very cruel to me." Gracie was so shocked by her statement that she wasn't sure what to say. "I'll expect you to be back in the morning, Gracie. And then we'll talk about your behavior."

"Good-bye, Cora. Don't call me again."

After hanging up, she sat there in her tent and wondered how her sister had gotten so high and mighty about herself. When her cell phone rang again, Gracie directed the call to voice mail then turned her phone off.

She'd not turned her phone back on once since then, preferring to use a pay phone with a card to call her mom and find out how she was enjoying herself. Neither of them mentioned Cora, and it was never brought up how they were going to live when they got home. They both, by silent mutual agreement, decided that the times they spoke were for them.

Gracie wiped at the tears that she'd thought she was done shedding. While she was having a wonderful time, she did miss having someone to share it with.

Pulling out her journal, she wrote what she was feeling and what things she had seen today. She was nearly finished with the entry when she heard a branch break very close to where she was.

Gracie wasn't a fool; she had a gun and a permit to carry

it. And she'd taken a lot of self-defense classes over the years. She could fight with the best of them. There was also a knife in her pocket at all times, and one in her boot. Her job as a freelance detective had given her a lot of moves that most people never got to learn.

The kid—he couldn't have been any more than about seven or eight—stepped out into the clearing where she was. He hadn't seen her yet, at least she didn't think so, but she watched him all the same. There was no reason for her to believe that he was as innocent as he looked, nor that he was alone. When he saw her, Gracie pulled out her gun and put it just under her leg. She never took chances.

As he made his way to her, she was careful to look around to see if anyone was following him. When he simply sat down on the edge of her sleeping bag, she just stared at him. For a kid, he was very brave.

"Do you have any idea where I am?" It was on the tip of her tongue to tell him that he was with her, but she didn't think he'd get the humor. "I've been lost for hours. And my phone don't work."

"Doesn't. And I have GPS on my tablet, but all I can tell you is that we're in Ohio. Are your parents camping too?" He told her no, they lived close by. "But you don't know where you are?"

"I have Peck, but he's been called away. I think he might have lost me too." Gracie offered him a bottle of water. "Thanks. I should have been smarter and not left the place where we were. I think they're going to be really worried about me."

"I'm sure they are. I don't have a phone that works anymore." She had one, but had had it cut off a few days ago when Cora would call and leave her so many messages that she'd not be able to get through them all. And then there was the added fact that it was hard to charge it when out here. "Do you know which direction Peck went?"

His pointing straight up didn't help. "He told me to stay where he'd left me, but I had to pee and I got all turned around when I went back. I'm pretty sure I'm going to die out here and they'll never find me." She wanted to laugh; the kid could do drama pretty good. "Do you think you can help me?"

"Sure. But as I said, I don't know this area any better than you do." He nodded and laid back on the grass. "Do you remember what time it was when you left home?"

"Nine-thirty. I ate and then Peck and I decided to have an adventure." He turned his head and looked at her. "Is that what you're doing? Having an adventure?"

"I am, as a matter of fact. I've been walking since I left my home over a month ago. I had no idea how out of shape I'd been before that." He nodded and closed his eyes. "Hey, kid, we have to get you back. No napping right now."

As she gathered up her things again, he helped her. Mostly by being in the way, but he did tell her that she'd left her knife on the ground. As they made their way in the general direction he'd been coming from when she'd seen him, he told her who he was and about anything else that popped into his head.

"My name is Mark Herald. Not for long though. My mom is dead; her name was Lynne. So is my dad. His name was

Robert. My mom killed him because he was going to burn a bunch of women on a stick." Gracie thought that someone should curb this kid's television watching time. "I've been living with Lelani, Shane, and Keion for a month now, and they want to adopt me. I can't wait."

"I bet you can't." Gracie pulled out her compass and looked at the sky. "I really wish I had a better way to get you home, buddy, but since you don't know where that might be, we could be walking in the wrong direction. I've been out and about for so long, I don't even think I'd remember how to drive a car. I'm sowing my wild oats at thirty."

"It's all right, we're going okay. I remember that rock over there." Which to her looked like every other rock in the forest. "I'm hungry too."

She handed him a candy bar and ate the last one she had for herself. Her plan had been to find a nice body of water, take a long bath, then go fishing. A week ago she'd done that and hadn't enjoyed a finer meal in all her life. Gracie asked Mark where a lake or pond was.

He had no idea, he told her, and she suddenly found herself being tossed away from him and the kid being dragged away by.... Well, she wasn't sure what it was. Standing up and trying her best to ignore the pain in her ribs and head, she pulled her gun out and shot three times at the thing. When he dropped Mark, she moved to stand over him as the thing stood up on its hind legs and roared at her.

If she remembered her mythology correctly, what was standing there was a griffin. But her mind kept telling her they were mythical. As in not real. Yet here he stood, glaring at her as if she'd taken his toy away.

"Don't move." Sounded like good advice, and she started to turn to see who had spoken to her. "He'll attack you again if you move. Right now he can't see you very well. Smell you either, for that matter. You're downwind from him."

He was mostly lion, the creature in front of her. His body, tail, and hind legs were very lion-like. However, he had wings and the head of an eagle. And his front legs were large talons of the same eagle. She'd read in college that the griffin was thought to be the king of all creatures, and guarded a treasure along with some priceless possessions.

"He came out of nowhere. I think Mark is hurt pretty badly." The man told her he'd be fine for now. "For now? You mean, he could eventually die?"

"I'm going to shift. But don't freak out or run. I have enough going on with Herbert here, and running after you is not going to make me very happy." He sounded bossy, like her sister, and when she turned to look at him, she fell back on her ass.

The dragon was staring at her like she was.... "Are you going to eat me? Or burn me...? Mark said that his dad was burning people on a stick. Are you his dad?"

Nothing. But when he took a step in her direction, she pointed her gun at him. Gracie had no idea whether it would keep him back or not, but she wasn't going to just lay here and hope he didn't have her for his dinner. But he turned to the large beast that had attacked them in the first place and roared at him.

Moving quickly, she made sure that Mark was all right. His head had a nasty bump on it, and there were some cuts on his face and arms, but it was the bite mark on his leg that concerned her. It was deep and wide. She was pulling out her first aid kit when she realized that the griffin and the dragon were both gone.

~~~

Shane felt his knees go weak when he saw his son. Christ, they'd been looking for him for over three hours, and not even the earth had been able to find him. Then Keion had heard the roar of something and said he was going to investigate. And a few minutes later, he'd told him where to find Mark. And a woman.

She was wrapping gauze around Mark's leg when he got to them. When she lifted her gun up and pointed it at him, Shane stopped. The first thing he noticed was that she was as comfortable holding it as she was administering aid to his son.

"My name is Shane Benson. That's Mark, my son." She asked him what his dead mother's name was. "Mine is Sally, his is Lynne. She committed suicide a few weeks back."

The gun went down but not far from her. "He was hurt. I'm not even going to tell you what did it or what saved our asses. Just suffice it to say, I'm going to go and see someone after this."

"You're hurt." She didn't say anything, but he did go to his knees by Mark. "Keion said that he'd been bitten, but he didn't know how badly."

"I don't know who that is. Other than the kid and the.... Other than the human kid here, I've not seen anyone else." She wasn't going to believe him, so he said nothing. "You should

187

be able to move him. He has a nasty bump on his head, but I think there's no bleeding there. And as I don't have the means to stitch him up, I did tape the wound together a little so he'd stop bleeding. I cleaned it as best I could as well."

When she stood up, he did as well. "Are you leaving? Now? I thought you'd wait here for the truck and we'd go back to my home. You have done us a big favor by helping out Mark." She picked up her backpack and he reached for her, just to touch her, when she drew her gun again. "I wasn't going to hurt you."

"No, you weren't." She backed up and Shane watched her carefully. It bothered him on a lot of levels that she didn't trust him. "The kid, I didn't hurt him. Something came out of the woods and knocked us both down."

Keion spoke to him through their link. *She has three broken ribs and a concussion. Also, I don't know how bad it is, but she has something wrong on her back. She winces when she has to bend.* He told him she was leaving. *I'd not let her if you can help it. The woman saved Mark's life by not letting Bolrock get him.*

Did you find out why he attacked him? Keion wasn't very happy as he explained. Shane actually thought it was funny, but decided to share with the woman to see if he could get her to stay. Or at the very least, let him touch her so they could form a link.

"Bolrock, the griffin that attacked, he did so because he didn't realize who Mark was when he peed against a tree in his territory. It's mating season for them, and he—"

"There are more than one of those things?" Her face bloomed in embarrassment. "Whatever. I'm out of here. I'm glad the kid is going to be all right."

188

"But you're not, are you? Broken ribs, a concussion? What if you get sick? Who is there to care for you?" Her footsteps back faltered a little and he took the chance to rush her. But the gun firing and the bullet slamming in the grass between his feet stopped him. "I just want to help."

"You just might want to think about living too." The truck coming from the right distracted him a little, and when he turned back, she was gone. Not just gone, but he didn't even see her on any path.

By the time they were able to get Mark awake and check out his wounds, an hour had passed. He and Keion went looking for her, his other half flying the skies, but they found nothing. No trace of a car, no tent that Mark told them she had bundled up, nor any kind of help from the earth. It was as if she simply disappeared.

Finally giving up on finding her as the sun went down, they headed back to the house. Mark was still awake when he and Keion went to see him. Peck was beside himself with concern, and had asked twice if they wanted someone else to care for him.

"No, you and Mark are good for each other. I understand that you told him to stay put, but he didn't." Shane looked at Mark, who had lowered his head in shame. "Next time, you'll both know better. And when you leave the house from now on, please make sure that your phone is charged."

"I will, I promise. Did you find the girl yet? She said that her phone wasn't working either. I thought maybe she could come here and get it charged up." Shane told him that they'd looked but she was gone. "She told me that she was sowing her oats. I'm not sure what that meant, do you?"

"She wants to get out and be free. Did she tell you her name?" Mark said that he didn't think so, but he did admit that he'd done most of the talking. "Well, we'll keep an eye out for her. Maybe tomorrow we'll have better luck."

When he made his way downstairs, he found Keion in the kitchen all alone. Sitting down across from him, he asked where Lelani was. He shrugged and said he had no idea. Keion looked up when he snapped his fingers in front of his face.

"Bolrock said that the woman shot him three times for no good reason." Shane said attacking Mark was good enough reason for him. "He said that she was the first human that he had ever tasted, and he would like to find her again."

"Did he say why?" Keion said that he hadn't, but it worried him. "Yes, it does me as well. Do you think he'd hurt her? For trying to protect Mark?"

"I don't know. I mean, I'd like to think he won't, but he was pretty upset with her. None of his wounds are life threatening, but he was upset." He stood up. "I'm going to take a walk. I need to find her. She's out there all alone and hurt."

Shane let the rest of them know what was going on and helped Roger with dinner. Lelani said she was working on something for the woman and would be late coming in. He asked to join her.

"If you can behave." He smiled. "I'm serious, Shane. I want to find her for what she did. Keion told me he's out looking as well."

"I'll behave. I might not like it, but I'll try. Roger will stay with Mark and Peck is beside himself with worry. I'm thinking he'll not let the boy out of his sight for a long time after this." Lelani laughed. "I'm not kidding. It wouldn't surprise me if he ended up showering with him. I've never seen anyone so upset before. My dad, he said he was going to take him out when he was better to show him how to find his way home. He did the same for us."

After she told him where she was headed, he explained to Roger where they were going. Grandda, as his Rottweiler, was going to help them as well. It was an all-out search for the woman and he was sort of nervous. He had a feeling that if she didn't want to be found, she wouldn't be.

Chapter 11

Jacob was really proud of the new castle. He'd never been in the old one but for the one time, and he thought that this place was just as nice. He knew from talking to Asher and the others that it was stronger. He sat down on the large bench nearest to him and leaned back. He was a mite on the tired side. When Essie came to sit next to him, he smiled at her and reached for his granddaughter. She was getting bigger every day.

"We're going to have a huge cookout. What do you think?" He told her that he could always eat something. "Yes, I love that about you. And since I have you here, I want to talk to you about living here with us. The other brothers have said that they're going to stay in their homes. And Simeon and Akassa are going to take over the house. But you have to live here with us."

"I don't know, sweetheart. I just don't feel right doing that." She asked him why and he leaned over to kiss his little Sally Anne before answering her. "You know as well as I that I was never meant for this kind of living. I mean, it's beautiful and all, but it just wouldn't feel right. Not by myself."

"Dad, plenty of people are going to be here. Asher is working on getting some of the people around town, ones that need a job, to come and help out. We've even hired a new cook so that Grandda has more time to do the things he wants." Jacob nodded but didn't tell her that she had it wrong. "Tell me, Dad. Please? Why won't you come and stay here with us?"

"Memories." He felt silly for saying it, but she wasn't letting go. "I have no memories of this place but bad ones. Of course, I did get my own Sally out of this, but there was nothing else. That house over yonder? It was where we lived, had our boys and raised them up. Both of us even passed on in that big house. I have no memories here."

"You could make some. With us." He'd thought of that too and told her. "I understand, I do. But I love having you with me. Knowing that if I need a breather, you're right there to take over with Sally Anne. Lindsey said she'd come to depend on you a great deal to watch over Eve Marie too."

He knew that too. But as much as they thought he was doing them a favor by keeping an eye on the little girls, they were actually doing him one. To think, after all this time, he was holding a little baby again.

When Essie was called away, he sat there with the baby just telling her about her grandma and stories of her dad and uncles. He thought that was the best part of having them around. Someone to hear his stories and not complain about how he'd told them that one about a million times.

"If that grandma of yours was here, she'd be teaching you how to knit up some of your own booties and things." He laughed. "Grandma sure does wish she could touch you two. Just yesterday when I was talking to her, she said she wanted someone to show you how to bake up some cookies and things."

Not quite true. What she'd told him was that she thought he was eating a lot of cookies and perhaps might do well to cut back a bit. But who was he to turn down one when they were offered up for him? Jacob didn't want to hurt anyone's feelings on this.

"And that cousin of yours? He cannot wait to get you two out where he can show you our exploring. We went down to the king and queen's tomb just the other day, and he was as good as gold when we got there. Told me that he liked it there, it was soft." Jacob liked it, too, and it was a good way to describe the peace that he got when he was there. "You two, I think you and Eve Marie are going to be a handful, and I cannot wait."

The longer he sat there, the longer his tales became. He'd caught great whales in the pond near the house. He'd climbed the mountain to pick cherries before anyone got up to know he was about. Jacob even let on that he might have singlehandedly got mates for all his boys.

"Do you normally tell lies to someone that cannot refute you?" He smiled at Lelani. She was a hard nut to crack, but he sure did love her. "I'm to tell you that you're staying here in this house. Actually, I was supposed to convince you of it, but I'm not any better at that than I am at being kind to strangers."

"You sent here by which one of them?" She told him and sat down. When he offered her Sally Anne, she told him no. Just like that, no. Jacob secretly thought she was afraid of the babies, but wasn't brave enough to find out. "You tell Asher that I was making my own decisions long before he got to put that crown on."

"Yeah, I'll do that. Not today. He's in too good a mood. I'll do it when he's all pissy. He can do pissy better than anyone I know." She leaned back in the big easy chair. This room, the library, was filled with books older than he was. Some new too, but not a great deal of them. And chairs that were so soft and comfortable when he sat in them that he usually took a nap. "I wanted to ask you something about before. About the time of my mom and sister."

"You go on ahead and ask away. If I know the answer, you know that I'll tell you." She nodded, but seemed to be taking her time in asking him. "When we first moved to the house down the road, did you know that there was nary a garden around? And there were few people that we could trust to get it plowed up for us. Then one day, we came out of the house and there was a hand plow, and also a big dray horse. I'll tell you, we had us a big wonderful garden for the rest of our days."

"Elbert still has it out in the barn. He said it's turned more dirt than a grave digger had. But this family, my mom told me once that you and Miss Sally had a man working here. It would have been about the time she was killed. That he was just a human and he was off in his head, she said. However, she had no idea what he was. I think, and this might be wrong, but I don't think my mom could tell the difference between someone human or not, even by touch."

"Let me think on that. And while I am, you tell me what you have going on. If you don't mind." She said that she didn't mind, but she thought perhaps she might have run across something that belonged to his family while she'd been in town. She'd been window shopping for something for the garden for Essie and had gone into the pawn shop. "Cain. He was the oldest boy of one of the men who had worked for the castle. Might have been killed that day too, I don't rightly know, but Cain, he couldn't talk much. Had him a bad case of the stutters if I remember correctly. But he could cane a chair faster than anyone that I ever met. What makes you think this person is part of his line?"

"I work with old tapestries; I think I told you that." He nodded. "Well, I was looking at one that they had in the window of the shop and I went in to ask them where they'd gotten it. Turns out that someone had left it there when no one could figure out what it was worth, if anything. The man, he told them they could have it then, he'd find something else to sell. I think perhaps it might be one that was here in the castle at one time. It depicts a farm with a great dragon in the sky. A pair of them actually, but one is on the ground."

"Can you tell for sure if you can get your hands on it?" She said that she already had. "So you're for sure that it belonged here? And these people, you thinking they might have pilfered it after the fall or something?"

"Or something. I'm not sure, but according to the story that the man said was told to him, the king had given it to this person's family when a child had been born. But that when the child had been born with a defect, which as you know could have been about anything back then, they tried to return it to the castle when the child had been put out." Jacob asked why the connection to this boy. "Story is that he was a wild child when he came here, and that you and Sally had given him something he'd never had. My mother thought that you should have drowned him like unwanted kittens, but then you know how she was."

"Sally was forever taking in anything and everyone that needed a little lift. For years I would think she was going to be murdered in her outings as she called them, but knew what most didn't; she was stronger than she ever looked." Jacob looked at her. "Like you. To see you right now one would think that you'd be an easy target. But I know better."

"I'm not an easy target." He laughed. "Anyway, if this boy was that man, then the tapestry should be repaired and given back to the man. It's worth hundreds of thousands of dollars, even for the condition that it's in now. Thomas, the owner of the pawn shop, he said the man was really down on his luck."

"And if you repair it? That's what you're thinking, isn't it? To have it repaired for them?" She nodded. "How much, darling?"

"Millions. And I'd gladly pay that for it for the chance to work on it for the castle. While they have a great many things that the queen and king saved for them, there is nothing that was in the castle that night, during the siege." Jacob nodded,

198

wondering why she'd want to help this man's family. "His name was Cain and he was kind to me, Jacob."

Her voice had gone sad, low but full of sadness. Jacob wanted to ask her what he'd done for her, how he'd touched her this way, but he wasn't sure that she'd tell him for one thing, and Jacob wasn't sure he wanted to know either. Whatever the memory was for her, it was painful and he didn't want her to hurt over it.

"You let me do some digging around, and I'll talk to Daniel too. He has more history on this area than even Elbert does." She thanked him and stood up. "This kindness that he did for you, can you tell me if he was hurt from it? He just disappeared one day, never to return."

"He was killed. Saving my life."

He nodded and she did as well. When she was gone, leaving him there with the sleeping baby, he pulled her to his heart and held her tight enough that she fussed at him. Looking down at her, her face so much like her momma's, he had to hug her once again. Tomorrow he was going to take the girls to see their grandmas again.

~~~

Getting out of the bed proved much harder than she'd thought it would be. Winter had settled in overnight and Lelani was pretty sure that snow was going to hit them soon. And being between two men that she loved more than she did anyone or anything else made it too tempting to just stay where she was. But she had something to do. And today, it had to be today.

It had only just occurred to her last evening that it was

199

her birthday today. To think just how old she was kind of depressed her a little. To have lived so many lifetimes, and she thought about all the people she had met and lost. Friends, there had been few of them, but they had meant a great deal to her at the time.

Lelani made her way to the kitchen and waited as Roger not only handed her a thermos of hot tea, but a heavy leather sack, as well as a blanket. The sack had been hers, given to her for one of her thousands of birthdays by someone that had meant all the world to her. Lelani asked him where he had found it. But then she realized that she shouldn't have been surprised…he had been with her forever, it seemed.

"You have had that look in your eye for days now. And I also know what this date is. You have not told them, have you?" Lelani shook her head. "I shall keep the men here while you do what you must. I know as well what was done for you. You go, talk to her. Remind her of the love that she told you of, and that you've found it finally."

"No one was ever better to me. Never treated me as she did." He nodded and hugged her to his warm body. "I had no idea that she'd passed."

"Nor did I, my lady. Had we known, perhaps we could have come to see her a final time." She nodded. "Go. Go now before I get weepy. T'would do us no good to be found here in the kitchen sobbing like this."

Making her way to the little cemetery, she wasn't surprised to find herself alone. Jacob spent a good deal of his morning here and sometimes late in the evening. But today, she had risen even before him. The sun wasn't yet up; the moon still gave the sky a nice glow. Thanking the earth for such a bounty of light enough to see by, she pulled out the warm scone she'd been able to smell in the kitchen. Eating it as she walked, she thought of the woman buried here.

Sally Benson had been someone…actually the only person that she'd ever trusted. Not just with her love, which until recently Lelani thought her incapable of feeling again, but also to trust. Sometimes in her life that was the most difficult thing for her to do.

Spreading out the blanket on the cold ground, Lelani put her hands to the earth and asked for forgiveness, but asked for a little warmth. Not only did the ground around her warm, but the air was warm enough that she could no longer see her breath. Laying out the things in the sack, she took her time with setting them along the headstone, telling the woman there what she remembered about it.

"I have no idea why you took me into your heart. And you told me over and over that you did love me. It took me awhile to realize the feelings that I had for you were love, but you were so patient with me. To this day I think of the advice you gave me, things to remember on how to cool my temper. I will admit that over the years I've lost the art of doing that. Sometimes, most of the time, it's easier for me to hate than it is to risk having my heart ripped from my chest again and again." She picked up the first item. "I was ten when you gave me this one. I treasured it for months after when I found it. Still do, I guess. The note, I'm afraid, has long since been destroyed. Moving as I have, it couldn't last."

The small doll, made from scraps of this and that, had been so wonderful to find with the ribbon tied around her waist that she'd thought it left by someone richer than her, and had been careful not to touch it at first for fear of being arrested. She had thought her mother would have put it out there to trick her into having to give it to her sister. Then she'd beat Lelani for taking it.

Her straw hair was a little worn in places, missing in others, but was still yellow and soft. The dress had more than likely been made from Sally's sons' clothing; it was dark and the buttons too large for the size of the clothing. The face on her was stitched to be a happy one...red thread that made a smile, blue for the eyes. There were even little freckles on her cheeks.

"I had left it there the first day because I was fearful that Mother would accuse me of stealing it. I couldn't read then, not well, but I knew that the first letter was what my name was, so I came to take it. For several days after, I would go back, having not played with it at all, waiting for someone to take it back." Laying the little doll in front of the headstone, she continued. "Mother never knew about us. No one did. I was careful, as you told me, to come only when your boys and husband were away. Picking mushrooms with you gave me so much. Not just food in my belly when you'd bring me things, but how to find other foods in the forest that I could eat."

The second item that she pulled from the bag and placed on the headstone was a book. It too was worn; its cover was nearly worn to the pages in some places. The binding on it had been coming off, so she learned how to repair it and had done the work herself. The book, like the other things, had kept her from harming herself over the years. Just the thought

202

of the woman that had given them to her had been enough.

"You must have known that I wasn't able to read this. But you helped me with that as well, didn't you? No one had bothered to help me read or write. And numbers were as much a mystery to me as the workings of my body." She thought of how Sally, a woman with six sons, had given her all the information to go from child to woman so that she'd not be alone in that as well. "I found the notes attached to different things. A tree with the word on it. There was a rose with a drawing, as well as the way it would be spelled out. I might not have been able to read big books, but the one you gave me became easier and easier after that. And now I can read as well as any scholar, and understand even more."

In a gentle way, Sally Benson had taught her not only to read, but to be adventurous as well. Finding the notes, the drawings, as well as learning something as magical as the written word, had kept her grief at bay. Her mother was gone; her sister had shunned her. Even the people in the town had very little to do with her. Lelani figured out later, decades later, that it had more to do with the fact that she looked like her sister so much, not because of who she was. For she doubted that anyone knew of her.

There had been other items, but many had long since been eaten or worn out. There had been a pretty dress, the first one she'd ever owned that wasn't a cast off from her sister. A ribbon for her hair that she'd lost once when she'd forgotten to remove it before going into the house. Her mother had beaten her but good for her not telling her where she'd gotten it, but Lelani never did. It was hers and given to her with love. There had been blankets, warm coats. Knitted hats and gloves. All treasures to her and cherished more than anyone could have guessed.

"When Jacob told me that he'd never known about me, I was hurt. You and I, we had so much together that I was injured that you'd not told him. Then I thought about how much we had shared, how you and I would talk quietly, how you'd listen to my heartbreak. It was then that I realized that what we did, how we'd meet, was more special because of that." She pulled out the next item and flattened it out on the grass so she could remember more. "You made this for me. I know that you'd made the boys all a sweater that year as well. I wore mine when I was not only cold from the weather, but when I needed the warmth of your love. Had it not been for this sweater, knitted by you for me alone, I would have found a way to have ended my life. Even in the darkest of times this would bring me comfort like nothing else could."

She laid the sweater — worn at the elbows, the neck of it stretched out, the color faded now that its age was countless to her — over the woman who had given it to her. The ribbon around it with another note, another declaration of love, was still there as well. Lelani kissed her fingers and took them to the sweater. She wished that she could, one more time, hug the woman who had been more of a mother to her than her own had been.

"I don't know how you found out that it was my birthday. I mean, I did figure it out and for a time, I thought that you were feeling sorry for me. That you were making these things for me because you knew that no one else would have cared. There wasn't anyone around to wish me well. For a brief moment in time, someone loved me for me. And you gave me that, Lady Sally." She pulled out the small tin and opened it now. The last thing that she'd received from the woman who had not only loved her when no one else had, but had kept her alive, quite literally. "When you passed, I grieved for months. I wasn't here when you died…I was far away, licking my own wounds when I'd been hurt by Erin. After I heard I came here nightly, just to sit with you, talk to you. Jacob's passing hurt me as well. You talked of him so much, and your boys, that I felt as if I knew them as well as I did myself. I have…. Oh Sally, I have missed you so very much."

When she'd gotten the tin, it had been filled with a scone and a small gauze bag filled with a fragrant tea. There had been a cup as well, long since broken, but a piece of it was now in the little box that had held the other things in it. The gauze bag, dark with the stain of the tea, still lay in the bottom with the string attached.

Lelani had gone to the creek by the cave where she'd been staying to get water. Because of Sally, she'd been able to not only start a fire, but she was able to find enough sweets of the earth to have a sweet cup of tea like a proper lady. She'd used the tea up, having several cups of the brew, each taste of it weaker as she used it, but no less wonderful for her.

The tin was also now filled with dried petals that had been laid upon Sally's grave. They'd once been roses, blue as the sky during a storm, but were now only reminders of the worst day of her life.

A mushroom from the garden that Sally had picked from the very day that she'd gotten sick was in the tin. There was also the knife that had forever been in Sally's pocket when she'd gone out. Lelani had found it in the mushroom garden a month after Sally's passing. Treasures she knew that meant everything in the world to her.

"When I left this area, the pain of you gone being too much for me to bear, I also left my sister. You said that I needed to spread my own wings, to get out and find my own path, so I did. I would see her on occasion, talk to her; or rather, have her tell me what she was doing, what she was accomplishing. But she never asked about me, as you said she wouldn't, nor did she care that I was still alive. Hoping, I guess, that I was as dead and cold in the ground as our mother." Lelani thought of her own mother now, the blood of her blood. "Erin had her killed. I know that now. And I think, as you told me, she would eventually get around to doing the same to me. My power and hers, it was what she wanted all along, something that was gifted to me over her."

Lelani laid on the grave now, no longer caring that it was cold around them. The woman here, the only person that had ever loved her all those years ago, was close now, and she could talk to her when she wanted. Lelani knew that she would too, that she'd come out there to talk to her, tell her things of her day, memories that she was making. And stories of her new son.

"I love Shane and Keion. They're so good to me, giving me everything that I ever wanted, some that I never realized I would. You raised them all to be good men, caring and loving. And I think you'd love Mark as well. Taking him in, it mellowed me a great deal. Makes me think of my words in the event that he should hear them." She fingered the ring on her finger, thinking of all the changes in her life, both now and then, that were because of Sally Benson. "I love you, Sally. I miss you so much and love you with all my heart."

Closing her eyes, she let the tears flow down her cheeks and onto the earth below her. There was no need for her to quiet her sorrow so she let it go, sobbing out the pain of her loss that she'd held so tightly to her for too long. As she laid there, her heart hurting, her mind full of memories, she heard the hard crunch of the frozen earth breaking, felt the arms of love wrap around her, and hoped that she'd come home. That Sally had somehow known she was there and had come to hold her again.

Before You Go...

HELP AN AUTHOR

write a review

THANK YOU!

Share your voice and help guide other readers to these wonderful books. Even if it's only a line or two your reviews help readers discover the author's books so they can continue creating stories that you'll love. Login to your favorite retailer and leave a review. Thank you.

NOW AVAILABLE IN THE DRAGON'S SAVIOR SERIES

COMING SOON

AWARD WINNING, BESTSELLING AUTHOR

Kathi Barton, winner of the Pinnacle Book Achievement award as well as a best-selling author on Amazon and All Romance books, lives in Nashport, Ohio with her husband Paul. When not creating new worlds and romance, Kathi and her husband enjoy camping and going to auctions. She can also be seen at county fairs with her husband who is an artist and potter.

Her muse, a cross between Jimmy Stewart and Hugh Jackman, brings her stories to life for her readers in a way that has them coming back time and again for more. Her favorite genre is paranormal romance with a great deal of spice. You can visit Kathi on line and drop her an email if you'd like. She loves hearing from her fans. aaronskiss@gmail.com.

Follow Kathi on her blog: http://kathisbartonauthor. blogspot.com/

www.ingramcontent.com/pod-product-compliance
Lightning Source LLC
Chambersburg PA
CBHW032124170626
46808CB00006B/2094